Boyfriend Maintenance

A FAKE RELATIONSHIP ROMANCE

LAUREN HELMS

Lauren Helms

Published by Lauren Helms (www.authorlaurenhelms.com)

Images © DepositPhotos – palinchak & 4pmphoto

Cover Design © Designed with Grace

Editing by JL Anderson (TheAverillScribe.wordpress.com) and Judy Zweifel (www.judysproofreading.com)

Formatting by Katy Ames

To Leigh, MK, Allie, Kay, Aubree, Sylvia, Katy, and Claire.
You took a chance with me and because you did, the journey has been
amazing.

BOYFRIEND MAINTENANCE

Emmy

My bad reputation is coming back to haunt me. Now, I need a date for my brother's wedding just to keep the vultures at bay. I've noticed Jake around the building and he's the perfect man for the job.

The thing is, I don't actually have what I promised in return for his help, but I don't want this to end.

Jake

I've seen Emmy and she's out of my league, but that doesn't stop me from taking her up on her offer and upping the ante. I have rules, however, the more time we spend together the more the lines get blurred. Her lie made her more like me than I ever thought possible. Too bad liars don't do it for me.

A little boyfriend maintenance goes a long way...

After all, 425 Madison Ave is the perfect place to fall in love!

∼

Each story in the 425 Madison Series is a complete standalone. For more information on the series please visit www.425madisonseries.com

PLAYLIST

'Welcome to New York' - Taylor Swift

'Suit and Jacket' - Judah & the Lion

'Sit Still, Look Pretty' - Daya

'Connection' - OneRepublic

'Broken' - lovelytheband

'Delicate' - Taylor Swift

'There's No Way' - Lauv featuring Julia Michaels

'Hurt Somebody' - Noah Kahan with Julia Michaels

'Find You' - Nick Jonas

'I Found' - Amber Run

'Out Of My League' - Fitz and The Tantrums

'Born To Be Yours' - Imagine Dragons, Kygo

To listen to the full playlist, check it out on Spotify and on YouTube!

CHAPTER 1

mmy

I'VE LIVED and breathed New York City my whole life. The hustle and bustle of
the only city I've ever known is calming. Sounds of sirens, impatient drivers
honking, constant pings of crosswalk lights, and chatter from the masses of
people that fill the sidewalks. All of these harmonize into the symphony of a city
that sings to my New Yorker heart. Even the city smell is enough to make me
smile on a bad day. The fragrances of different foods wafting from the street
vendors and coffee shops on every city block feed my city soul. The car exhaust
and body odor are no match for the smell of the wet concrete during a rain-
shower though. As much as I love the city life with the city streets that never
sleep, it can cause sensory overload.

Thankfully I have the mobile Digibot game in my pocket. This game. I
swear, my life would be so freaking boring if I didn't have it. Living in good old
New York City is a Digibot Go player's dream. The more populated an area is,
the more Digibot Go activity can be found. As a Digibot handler, I'm able to
catch and train over two hundred Digibots within the game world. There are
rewards for every step taken. The game has led people to experience new places

around the world by catching special Digibots and placing Digistops throughout the most popular places on the planet. Lucky for me, if I walk to work, I hit nine stops. It's all about the Digiballs, people.

After snagging a high-powered Digibot right outside my building, I slide my phone back into my purse. Ah, the perks of living in such a big, luxurious apartment building. Thirty-four floors high, 425 Madison offers a bazillion different amenities. Being the home of a Digistop, isn't on their website, but I sure as heck consider it a top selling point. The second I set foot into the 425 Madison building, the high-energy city fades away behind me.

"Good evening, Miss King," Thomas, the doorman, says with a smile. He backs up and reaches to get the door to let me into the building.

"It's a beautiful night, isn't it?" I smile at him.

"Just like you, Miss King."

I blush as I walk through the open door. He's a sweet man and I always look forward to seeing him each day, no matter whether I'm coming or going.

A light, Zen-like music plays overhead. It's so faint I can hear the click of my heels as I walk through the modern Art Deco lobby. 425 Madison exudes an unsurpassed level of swankiness.

Too bad I can't afford to own one of the units in this beautiful oasis of luxury.

No, I'm not a squatter. I am a paying resident, it's just that I pay my roommate Becca, who is also my best friend. She pays the rent on our chic little two-bedroom on the fourteenth floor. I cover our utilities.

Becca is what you would call a trust-fund kid. Her parents are old money, and her trust fund won't dry up any time soon. If it weren't for her, I'd be living in a studio apartment somewhere in Queens.

Speaking of my best friend, I spot her as she steps off the elevator. I raise my hand in greeting when she takes a sharp turn away from the front of the building. She's heading toward the leasing office.

Huh. She pays all her bills via online banking, so I'm not sure why she would need to visit the back office. As I get closer to the elevators, she's still in my line of sight. That's when I realize something looks off about her. My best friend, a five-foot-seven beach-blonde socialite who'd rather wear jeans and a trendy top than the latest, fresh-off-the-runway fashion, looks downright suspicious right now. Like she's up to no good. I catch her looking over her shoulder more than once; I come to a halt when I spot her leaning up against the wall before turning again, passing up the leasing office.

What the heck is she up to?

Curiosity gets the best of me as I follow her down the hall. In addition to the leasing office, the maintenance office and service elevator are also down this corridor. This is where the waitstaff and other employees access the building's rooftop lounge. I'm grateful the granite flooring has switched over to plush carpeting which silences the clacking of my heels in my stealth pursuit of Becca.

Copying her same position moments ago, I lean against the wall and listen.

"Oh, wow. It's so big."

My eyes go wide at what I hear come out of her mouth. A deep, male chuckle follows.

"I can't wait to get my hands on it."

What the heck?

"The balls just fit so perfectly in my hand."

I slap my palm over my mouth to trap the giggle about to bubble out of me. What in the world is she doing? I hear rustling, someone brushes up against the wall. Then the man she is with grunts. And to my surprise, another male voice chuckles in response.

There's two of them?

"Watch it, this cost me enough. I better get my money's worth, boys."

Oh, shit. Why would she need to meet these guys in secret, in the back of the building?

At the risk of catching my best friend in a secret lover's rendezvous, I slowly backtrack down the hall. Once I get a clear view of the lobby, I hightail it into an elevator. A couple minutes later, I'm unlocking my apartment door. I'm not even four steps in the apartment when I realize the living room has been reorganized. I'm totally alright with the new setup, but Becca normally talks to me before rearranging. Once I'm in my room, I kick off my heels and toss my purse on the dresser.

Sitting down on my bed, I dig my hose-covered toes into the soft, plush carpet and let out a relaxing sigh. I consider changing my clothes, but we have dinner plans tonight. Just then the front door opens, and I hear Becca barking directions. She's rather bossy tonight. I wonder if the boys downstairs didn't do it for her.

It's time to sort this out. Stepping into the doorway of my room, I see her standing in the entryway as two men push a massive ... thing wrapped in what looks like plastic wrap into our apartment.

"That's right, ease it in. You gotta ease it in so it fits ... just right."

So, she isn't saying these things in a sexual context, but damn. That's a lot of "what she said" jokes ready and waiting to be thrown out there.

"What's that?" I ask, coming to a stop next to her.

She jumps and her hand flies to her heart. She didn't realize I was home. "Ack! Em, what are you doing here?"

"I live here."

I can't tell what these guys just pushed in to our apartment. Whatever it is, it's huge and I doubt she's had it approved by management.

She places her hands on her hips and laughs sarcastically. "Yeah, I know. But what are you doing here right now? I thought you had to work late."

"Oh, yeah, they canceled my last meeting of the day, so I was able to get my work done."

Nodding, she looks back to the men, telling them to put it next to the wall, in the far corner of the room, she turns back to me with the biggest smile on her face.

"I have a surprise for you."

"Oh yeah? That thing?" I point to the machine.

"Yes, you know that childhood dream of yours?" Both of the men step back and admire their work.

"The dream where I become a pop princess and marry Justin Timberlake. Joey Fatone officiates our wedding, everyone chuckles throughout because it's the most entertaining ceremony everyone has ever been to?"

"No, the other, more attainable one." She turns to thank the men and follows them to the door to let them out.

Then it hits me.

"The one where I have a real, found-in-arcades-everywhere, Skee-Ball machine in my living room?"

She's nodding vigorously through a smile and clapping her hands in front of her chest.

I take a step, zeroing in on the giant, wrapped-up arcade game. "But how? Why? How much did this puppy cost?"

"I set up an alert a few months ago for a used one in good shape. This one came from a local arcade that is closing. So, I got a great deal on it. And as for why, it's simple. I love you and you've always wanted a Skee-Ball machine. I know you'll never buy one for yourself, so I'm doing it for you. I'm also like ninety-nine percent sure we aren't allowed to have this, so you can't tell anyone. I snuck it up here."

A moment later she's standing next to me with a pair of scissors, cutting away the thick plastic wrap. When we have it plugged into the wall, I pick up the brown, faux-wood ball. It fits perfectly in my hand, the cool plastic feel of the ball reminds me of Becca's earlier words, the ones I overheard in the hall. Chuckling, I roll the ball down the alley and it lands in the center fifty-point slot.

Hell yeah, that feels good.

ake

"OH, WELL ... HELLO THERE, HOT STUFF." Mrs. Jenkins stands in the open doorway of her apartment. Her arm slides up the doorframe slightly awkwardly as she leans into the frame. She's attempting to look sexy in a Japanese silk kimono robe. It's a red floral print that hangs nearly to her ankles. She has surprisingly good posture for a seventy-year-old woman.

Her husky voice is seductive as she gestures for me to come in. I have to mentally prepare myself every time I have a work order for unit 2007. Which is normally once a week.

Mrs. Jenkins is a retired Broadway actress. She hit her stride when she starred in the hit musical *Chicago* in the mid-seventies. Dorthy Jenkins is a dramatic, wealthy retiree who just happens to hit on me every time I'm here. She may be a tad lonely, so I deal with it.

"Good afternoon, Mrs. Jenkins. My work order says that you've got faulty smoke detectors." Honestly, that seems a bit suspicious since we worked through the entire building updating the detectors less than six months ago.

"Dorthy, darling. Please, stop calling me Mrs. Jenkins. You make me feel like a cougar."

I raise my eyebrow at that. More like a puma since she's got to be at least forty years older than me. I set down my toolbox and scan the living room for the unit's central detector.

"All right, Dorthy. You're having issues with the smoke detectors? Let's just take a look. I'll get these fixed up in no time." Really, I just want to get out of here. The longer I'm in this apartment, the more cheek pinches I get. And I'm not just talking about pinches to my face. She gets a little bolder with each visit. Not looking forward to the day she takes it too far. Her flirting seems harmless though. She just really appreciates those "hot young thangs." Her words, not mine.

"Well, no rush. I'll just pour us a little nightcap." I don't mention it's only four in the afternoon. "Will two fingers do, Jake? I've always preferred two." She waggles her eyebrows.

I divert my eyes. The sexual reference catches me off guard and I feel my face heat.

Clearing my throat, I shake my head. "I'm sorry, Dorthy, but no drinking on the job." I pull out my step ladder so I can reach the smoke detector.

"You're such a good boy, darling. I admire that. I'll just have a nip and enjoy the show."

Just like she normally does. Unfortunately, she isn't the only 425 Madison resident to watch me while I do my job. I've worked in this building for nearly three years now. Growing up, I never had dreams of becoming a maintenance man, but I've always been good with my hands. I was the man of the house, that somehow led me down a path of being the neighborhood handyman. Not having enough money for college, I found a job for a hotel working on their maintenance team. A few years ago, I snagged this job. The pay is a hell of a lot better. Since the building offers 24-hour maintenance, when I'm on call, I stay in a swanky one-bedroom unit on the third floor. It beats the hell out of my janky-ass studio apartment in Queens.

But I have to admit, I love my job. I like fixing things. I enjoy that every day is different. And there are a lot worse places that I could be stuck fixing up. The only downfall is that I get a front-row seat to the high-society life I'll never have. One I never want. I've always had to work for the money to pay for a roof over my head, the food I eat. Half of the people living in 425 don't even work. At least if they do, they don't work normal nine-to-fives.

Working here has allowed me to finally be in a good place financially, but I'm barely what you'd consider middle class. These residents though? They might not be the one-percenters, but they are clearly in the top fifteen. I'm not bitter. I just know my place. I'm content down here in the lower middle.

After unscrewing the faceplate, I twist off the cap of the detector. Sure enough, the battery is missing. As expected. It turns out the wires have also been cut. I shouldn't be surprised. Like I said, I'm up here on the twentieth floor visiting Mrs. Jenkins at least once a week. Ninety percent of the time it's not a true maintenance issue. In the past I've removed a complete roll of toilet paper from the back of the tank. There was that time I pulled out a purple dish towel from the garbage disposal. Then there was that time she jammed her bedroom window so it wouldn't close. I had to stand in her room, with her conveniently scattered old lady undergarments strewn all about and realign her window slides. It never ends with this woman.

"Well, Dorthy, it looks like the battery died. I'm going to have to replace it and a few other key parts. I've brought some with me, so I can take care of them now. I'm guessing the other two have the same issue." I climb down from the ladder and walk over to my bag. Squatting down, I try not to make eye contact with the woman who's spread out across her chaise watching me like a hawk ready to dive in for the kill.

"Oh, dear. Those darn batteries."

Yeah, those darn batteries and wiring will end up costing about a hundred and fifty to fix.

Fifteen minutes later I'm packing up my stuff. Thank god, I'm done here. This was my last job for the night and now I've got a nice two-day weekend. With a rare two days off I'll be visiting my mom over on the island and catching a Mets game with my brother, Kevin.

"Well, all done here, Dorthy. Hopefully, those new batteries work better for you. I'd hate for something to happen to them and us not be able to get up as quickly as I was able to today. When smoke detectors aren't working, it's a safety risk."

"Oh, Jakey-pooh, you're just too good to me. Always on top of things. Just the way a young buck like you should be." She reaches over and pats my ass as I walk past her out the door.

"Mrs. Jenkins, we've talked about this. You need to keep your hands to yourself." She just pouts and I know my gentle warning has fallen on deaf ears. "Have a good day, ma'am." And I close the door quickly, finally putting some much-needed space between me and the spinster.

I take my first relaxing sigh once the elevator door closes behind me and I'm safely headed back down to the maintenance office. My phone vibrates in my pocket. Pulling it out I see I have a notification for the hookup app I use.

Look, I work a lot. Five days a week, ten-hour shifts. If I don't work a full week onsite, I'm at least on call. I fill up my downtime from work watching baseball. I'm a born and bred Mets fan. I visit my mom over on Staten Island a few times a month and I have a few good friends that I hang out with when I can. I meet them for drinks at our favorite bar. I don't have a lot of free time outside of all that, so I don't have time to date. Mostly, I don't have time to meet women interested in sharing me with 200 other people and all their handyman needs. So instead, I just use the Match Me app for hookups. Occasionally, I'll meet up with the same woman twice, but most end up wanting more.

Opening the app, I see that I have five new matches for the day. I don't check the app regularly. Just when I need to get some.

What? Don't judge. I'm a hot-blooded twenty-nine-year-old living in the Big Apple. I've got needs. I swipe left on the first three, dismissing the matches. The fourth match is a woman in this building. I've seen her around. She carries around one of those small dogs, it's ugly as sin. Ah, unit 315. It's sad that I identify them by their unit numbers rather than their names. I refuse to bang any chick who lives in the building, but out of curiosity, I check out her profile since I can't, for the life of me, remember her name. Eliza Donovan. Ah, that's right. Sexy, dark hair, and short. I swipe left to get my fifth match.

A pretty blonde chick looking away from the camera. She's outside somewhere and her hair is blowing across her face. I can't tell if she looks familiar or if she's just got one of those faces. I read that her name is Sara and we're the same age. What the heck, I need to get laid. So, I swipe right. A few hours later, after several text exchanges through the app, we've set up a date to meet tomorrow night. It will be a spectacular weekend for sure.

CHAPTER 3

mmy

AFTER A FEW HOURS of brushing up on our Skee-Ball skills, we finally go to dinner. We love this little place called Ivy's. While it's open during the day for lunch through dinner, it's the perfect spot for late-night eats after a long day of work. It's got great bar food with a twist of upscale delight. It reminds me of college, when I was still living off my father's dime. Now that I'm living on my own and not the life I was born into, I try not to hang out in high-society haunts where I might run into people I grew up with.

The only person I still see and interact with from my childhood is Becca. We went to prep school together and have been joined at the hip ever since. She's the only person in my life who doesn't give me a hard time about not using my trust fund.

My father, he's confused, as well as annoyed, that I'm not living up to my potential as a King. My stepmother is just plain embarrassed. I have zero in common with my stepsister, Ashley, so I honestly don't know how she feels about me. I can't remember the last time we even had a conversation. Then there's my older brother. Levi is one of my favorite people. But even he doesn't understand why I won't live the King way.

My great-grandfather started King Cosmetics from the ground up more than a hundred years ago. The company has been passed down and now belongs to my father. It has always been the plan that Levi, being my father's only son, would take over for him someday. Levi has followed my father's plan, just as they have told him to. I don't know if it's something he truly wants for himself.

The plan for me was a lot simpler. I was to grow up to be a rich man's arm candy. Having my stepmother, Kitty, as my example of the perfect trophy wife, I quickly decided that wasn't the life for me. No, I wanted more than that. I wanted the world.

I didn't go to Harvard like my father had planned. I went to Cornell instead, for a degree in business and marketing. Good ol' Dad didn't love that decision, but he realized that, with a business degree, he'd be able to add another King to the company's board of directors someday. Little did he know, I never planned on working for him.

I knew I wouldn't have been able to pay for Cornell on my own, so I let my father pay for just one more thing. Upon graduation, I promptly cut myself off from my family-funded bank accounts and got a job with Envirogal. It's a smaller cosmetic company. It's 100% earth-friendly, non-animal testing, naturally beautiful makeup. I love the company and what they stand for. The owners and management are wonderful to work with. I know they hired me because of my name, but they quickly learned that they got way more than just the King name. While I might feed my dad the "I'm just gaining experience in my career" line, Envirogal and I both know that I will never work for King Cosmetics, and that I have no plans of leaving.

The day I cut myself off from the family money was both the scariest and most empowering day of my life. There was no more money. Only the money I had in the bank from my college paid internship. When I turned twenty-five and my trust fund became available to me, everyone thought for sure I would change my mind and join the dark side again. Nope. What came along with cutting ties to all that money were all the family expectations looming over me. My path was now clear, and I had every intention of following the Yellow Brick Road all the way to Oz. On my own time, in my own way.

My parents aren't happy with me. Even after six years. We've had a very rocky relationship since. Kitty has never shied away from letting me know how poorly I've run my reputation through the mud with her country-club set. Living the life of privilege isn't something to just throw away for a temper tantrum. Yes, she still thinks I'm throwing a tantrum.

Honestly, I love my life. I love the freedom that comes with making my own decisions without worrying about showing up on Page Six. My life is perfect because it's mine.

It's nearly nine when Becca and I get back to the apartment. A large group of people huddle outside the entrance to our building. Thomas, still manning the doors, doesn't seem concerned, so I assume somewhere in the group may be a resident or two. I've got my Digibot Go app pulled up on my phone. While Becca doesn't play the game, she's long past giving me grief over my obsession. I'm not ashamed to say that I'm obsessed with this newest internationally acclaimed mobile game, I just don't normally announce it from the rooftops. Which is why I slow down and come to a stop before Thomas greets us and opens the door.

When I'm done, I follow Becca into the building. Still looking at my phone, I'm distracted by an email from Kitty that pops up on my screen, I slam into a thick, warm brick wall.

Well, not really, but when I look up, I see that I've run smack into the maintenance guy here in the building, also known as Jake. I've never formally met him, we've only had a few issues in our apartment over the years, and when maintenance shows up, I'm always at work. But he's well known throughout the building. You should hear what some of those old birds say about what they'd like to do to him. The sauna is a hot spot for gossip.

"Oh my gosh. I'm so sorry. I wasn't paying attention at all." I shove my phone in my purse and step to the side, out of his way. He's taller than me. With my heels on, I'm about five-six", so he's at least six foot. His hair is cut short, but it's thick. I don't get any further in my perusal because I'm distracted by his chuckle.

"No problem, I wasn't watching where I was going either." He's smiling down at me and I can't help grinning back.

"Oh, well then I guess it was the perfect storm." Am I attempting to flirt? If so, I'm failing.

He laughs. "Yeah, guess so. Well, see ya." He winks and strides right on by me and out of the building. Watching his retreating form, I have a chance to check out his sexy-as-sin muscular backside.

"Ahem. Would you like something to wipe up that drool you got there on your face?"

I snap out of it and glare at Becca. "I'm not drooling."

"Right. And we don't have a Skee-Ball machine upstairs. Admit it, that man is probably as sexy as they come." She hooks her arm through mine and we walk through the lobby.

"You should ask him out." Becca eyes me as she jabs the button to call the elevator.

"What? No way." A confused look taking over my face.

"Why not? He's hot, you're hot. I bet he's damn good with those hands of his."

I shake my head. "He's probably got a girlfriend. Or a wife."

"No wife. I didn't see a ring." She's one of those people who has an answer for everything.

"Plus, I think I flirted with him. He didn't flirt back. So, he's probably not interested." I wonder out loud, Or maybe, I just suck at flirting.

"You'll never know if you don't ask him. I'd ask him out, but it wouldn't end well."

Cocking my head her way, I ask her why.

"Because the sex would be fan-fucking-tastic and then I'd take him home for Christmas and my parents would ask him what he did for a living. As soon as they found out he was the good ol' maintenance man they'd shit a freaking brick." Yeah, they probably would. Her parents would have totally betrothed her at age seven if that was still socially acceptable.

"We are cut from the same cloth, Bex. So why do you think I should date him?" The elevator door slides open.

She turns to me with a grin and walks into the elevator backwards. "Because you don't give a rat's ass what your parents think. So, you're free to fall in love with anyone you want."

"Whoa, who said anything about falling in love?" I follow her.

"Okay, screw. Screw anyone you want. Please, for the love of god, do that soon. You need to get laid."

Wow, thanks, dearest best friend.

I must mutter the words because she just laughs.

"Emmy, when was the last time you got laid?"

I bite my lip. I'm trying to think, and I can't stop the blush of embarrassment as I realize that I have to actually think so hard about when it was. Five months, maybe? Six?

"Somewhere between four and six months would be a safe guess," I tell her just as the elevator beeps, announcing its arrival on our floor.

"The fact that you didn't know the answer to that question is proof that you need to get a penis friend." Stepping off the elevator, she digs her keys out of her purse before I get the chance.

I choke on a snort. "A what?"

"A penis friend. As in you need penis. Bad." She waves me off like the words that just fell out of her mouth shouldn't surprise me. Then again, I guess they shouldn't.

"I've been busy," I offer up lamely.

"There's always time for sex." She looks back at me as she unlocks the door.

I shrug.

"No, Emmy, there is always time for sex. Make it a priority, please. You'll thank me for it afterwards."

"There will never be a time when I thank you for sex."

Bex replies by throwing her head back and laughing as I follow her in the apartment.

CHAPTER 4

ake

THE CAB DROPS me off right in front of a swanky-as-shit bar. Maybe the better term for it would be a cocktail lounge. Normally, you wouldn't catch me dead in a place like this, but it's my fault for not doing my due diligence before accepting Sara's location for drinks. But whatever. I've got a singular goal for tonight.

Walking into Blush, I quickly realize I have no business being here. This place is upscale. Good thing I always dress nice for these hookup dates because there is a dress code. The only nice clothes I own are a dark wash pair of jeans, black dress shoes, and a couple nice button-downs. I wear them so little that you can't tell they are a couple years old. I'm a jeans and T-shirt kind of guy. Work boots and sneakers. The doorman, a young twentysomething eyes me as I walk past him through the second set of doors.

Damn, these rich fucks are snooty. Hopefully, Sara and I can enjoy a drink or two and take this date back to my place. Or hers, which is actually the better option. Surprisingly, it's self-seating, so I find a small table for two near the door against the wall. The music playing overhead is instrumental, but the current song carries a familiar tune. The decor is glass and chrome and folded cloth napkins are placed at each table setting. I scan the lounge for a menu but no, you'll find no wall menu here. Too fancy.

"Well, hey there, sexy," a feminine voice says from next to me.

Uh.

I look up and the blonde with the nice smile from the Match Me app is smiling down at me. I stand to greet her. "Hey, Sara. How are you?"

She slides into my empty seat. Okay, odd, but whatever. I take a seat across the table.

"Hmmm. I love your warmth already." She wiggles into the chair as if she just can't get close enough to it.

"Uh," is all I can manage. She doesn't look crazy, but I'm not getting a good vibe here. And, as I assess her, I realize that she looks familiar.

"Jakey-pooh. You don't realize who I am, do you?" She waves a server over as she says this.

"It's just Jake. And should I know who you are? I mean, you do look familiar." Really, I can't place her face. But I know it.

She giggles. Just then the server arrives next to our table. She orders a Sex on the Beach and I order a Jack and Coke.

As soon as he leaves, she continues, "I figured you didn't know it was me, I mean, I've seen you several times since we set up this date and you haven't mentioned it," she pouts but continues. "I was kind of hoping it was because you were trying to keep things professional around the building. I get that, I really do."

Then it dawns on me. Fucking-a. She's a resident at 425 Madison. Damn it. Fifteenth floor.

"Ah, you are putting two and two together." She smiles.

Well shit. I'm not hooking up with anyone tonight it seems. "Look, Sara, I have a rule."

"Oh, like a safe word? That's a great idea. Do you have one you like to use, or can I pick it?" Her eyes are full of excitement.

I shake my head, I'm confused as to why we are on the topic of safe words.

"You know, I can see it now. You're into kinky. I bet you have a red room of pain. Oh my gosh, I'm so into red rooms." She claps her hands together in front of her and I'm completely at a loss for words. "I'm so excited. I mean, don't get me wrong, I've been wanting to check out that handyman you keep in your pants for a while now, but knowing that you're handy *and* kinky … I'm just about to burst." She winks at me then and adds, "If you know what I mean."

I clear my throat. This is nuts. She's crazy. It's not just me, right? I look around to the surrounding tables, hoping that others might have heard this conversation. Nope. No one is paying any attention to us.

"Look, Sara, I think we started off on the wrong foot—" I try to cut in but she's on a roll.

"You know, I'm really glad we did this. Normally, I like to jump right on in, you know the best foreplay in my book involves a lot of tongue and groping. But recently, I've realized the value of dinner or drinks beforehand. It allows us to get on the same page sexually." She starts to laugh. "See, had I just jumped you when I got here, I would have never known you preferred a little BDSM in the bedroom."

I can't take this anymore. "Sara, hold up."

"Oh my god, does this mean you're into anal?"

What the fuck?

I'm not sure when our drinks arrived, but mine is sitting within reach and I take a nice long gulp. She's going on and on about what sex positions she likes and wants to try. I slide my phone out of my pocket and shoot off a quick text.

A minute or two later, my phone rings. Thank god.

"Sara, can you hold that thought? My brother is calling. He knows I'm on a date, so I'm worried as to why he's calling." I answer my phone without giving her time to reply.

"Dude. It's that bad? I thought your date was at seven," Kevin says.

"Whoa, slow down, Kev. What's going on?" I fake my worry.

"Ha, shit, man. It's been a while since we've had to fake an emergency."

"Damn. Okay, thanks for letting me know, Kev, I'll be right there."

I hang up to his chuckling and give Sara my best disappointed look. "Sara, I'm so sorry to do this. But my grams, she fell again, and I need to get there to make sure she's all right." I pull out my wallet to fish out enough money for our drinks.

"Oh no, Jakey-pooh, I hope Grammy isn't hurt too bad. Do you want me to go with you?"

"No!" After nearly yelling, I clear my throat. Shit, get it together. "No, no, she really doesn't like new people, so if I have to take her somewhere, it's just going to be a long and stressful night."

She stands as I stand and I'm immediately worried about what she's about to do. She walks to me and kisses my cheek. I let out a breath. Thank god. But unfortunately, she doesn't stop there. She moves to my ear and licks it. She holds on to my shoulders and she sucks my earlobe into her mouth. Then she moans.

I gently push her way.

"Would you like me to hail you a cab, Sara?" I've now put a full chair length between us. I'm hoping she declines my offer, but I'm a gentleman, I don't want to leave her here.

"Oh, that's sweet, but I need to get laid tonight, so I'll stay."

Well then. She should probably add horny and honest to her dating profile.

I say goodbye and get the hell out of here.

"So, let me get this straight. She immediately started talking about getting down and dirty within the first five minutes?" Kevin sits across the table from me. He smacks his hand down on the dark wood table, throws his head back and laughs.

I roll my eyes as I take a pull from my beer bottle. We are at our favorite bar, Monterey's, after coming from the Mets game. It's a hole-in-the-wall place. From the street, it looks a little seedy, but one foot in the place and you immediately feel welcome.

"Oh, and Mom will get a kick out of your dick's new nickname. Little Handyman. Way better than Little Jake." The laughter in his eyes and the smile on his face makes it hard for me to really be mad at him for poking fun at my date with Sara the other night. I used him as a fake emergency, I expected as much.

"Dude, shut up. I haven't called him that since I was like seven." I shake my bottle a little to confirm it is indeed empty.

"Maybe so, but still. Mom will love hearing about this. I'm going to call her." He moves to pull out his phone from his pocket and I just give him a glare.

"Fine. I won't ... right now. But answer me this, big brother. Why do you refuse to sleep with any of the single ladies of 425 Madison?" He tips his bottle toward me.

"Simple. I don't want to shit where I eat." I can tell Kevin wants to razz on me more. So, I explain further. "Do you know how many times I go on a call and find myself being watched with lust-filled eyes? At first, it was flattering, but it's gotten old. I've just recently been able to reduce the amount of fake calls." I air quote that last part. "If word got out that I was open to the idea of sleeping with the residents, my calls would triple."

"Oh, poor Jake. Would you like some fucking cheese with that wine? Are you really complaining about all the women in your building enjoying a little eye candy while they wait for something in their apartment to be fixed?" He really doesn't get it.

"Yes, Kev. I'm really complaining. I'm not just talking about smoking hot twenty- and thirtysomethings. The teenage girls living in the building, married women, and even the Q-tips are all guilty of it. Hell, my week wouldn't be complete without some kind of sexual advance or come-on. Seventy-year-old Mrs. Jenkins is a repeat offender."

"I dunno, man, you're not that attractive." He leans back in his chair, crosses his arms over his chest and studies me.

"Pfft. Just last week, someone told me I could pass as a body double for one of the Jonas brothers." I brush the nonexistent dust off my shoulder.

Chuckling, Kevin reaches for his bottle of beer. "Fine. I might see it. Still, I think you're missing out on some hot and passionate resident sexy time."

"Whatever. Not going to happen." This isn't something I'm going to let up on. I don't want to mess with my job, a job that pays the bills and allows me to tuck some money away here and there for some high-society tail.

"Oh, that reminds me. My buddy told me that there is a house up for sale in Great Kills. He said it's a great starter home. You should check it out." Kevin knows I've been looking.

"Oh really? Any idea what they are asking?" I've been saving to buy a house on Staten Island for nearly two years now. That pesky down payment is keeping me from really getting serious with my realtor.

"I think like seven hundred thousand. Which isn't bad at all for that neighborhood."

"No, it's not. I'll have to check it out."

"Speaking of buying a house, how's that down payment fund coming along?" He motions to the server for another beer.

"Very slowly. I'm a little more than halfway there, but it's slow going." And so help me, if I have to put any more money into my apartment, then it's just going to slow me down even more.

"I don't understand why you are so hell-bent on buying a place on the island. Why not just get a better apartment, or buy a unit in a nicer place?"

"I need to be able to get out of the city. This place is crawling with tourists twenty-four seven and sometimes it's just nice to escape it."

"So, visit Mom more." He chuckles. "She would love that."

"I visit Mom plenty. No, I want my own place, away from the city that never sleeps. I *want* to fucking sleep once in a while. Preferably in a place that isn't in major need of fixing up. Even though growing up like we did—struggling to make ends meet, having that house in a friendly neighborhood—it's important to me. Someday, when I settle down and start a family, that's where I want to raise my kids. Not in the city. City kids are spoiled little shits."

He laughs at my last point. "Aw man, when you have kids, your little shits will be spoiled to hell by Mom, and you know it. It doesn't matter where you live, it's how you raise them."

I eye him. That was rather profound for a twenty-six-year-old with no goals of settling down anytime soon.

"Huh. Didn't know you were that deep, little bro."

"I'm as deep as the ocean. And if anyone knows what it's like to be raised in a shitty situation, it's us. But Mom raised us, and she did a fucking amazing job. And you know we would have turned out the same way whether we grew up in a shitty apartment in Queens, a high-rise on Madison Avenue, or the tiny three-bedroom on Staten Island."

Stunned by the revelation, I sit back in my seat. He's so fucking right.

"Shit. That's true. I feel like I need to buy Mom a medal or something." We both laugh. I run a hand through my hair and think about the larger than normal hug she's getting next time I see her.

"So, new plan?"

"Nope, I'm still buying a house on the island. Your revelation was good, but not that good."

He mutters something under his breath as I buy him another drink.

I've got a busy week ahead. I'm back on call for the next six days. Three of those days I'm on call overnight. So, after we make plans to meet up again for another game in a couple weeks, we go our separate ways.

CHAPTER 5

mmy

"Oh, hey, Olivia! I have some new samples for you. We were prepping for a trade show and just restocked our samples and all that fun stuff. I brought you some." I hand a small, Envirogal tote full of samples to her. I was planning on running it down to her apartment tonight after dinner, but since we are both checking our mail, it's perfect timing.

"Ooh, thank you, Emmy. You know how much I love this stuff. You're so good to me." She takes the bag and peers in.

"Of course, I'm just happy you finally found a line you love." I was talking to Olivia one day a few months ago in the gym about skin care. She wasn't loving her current products, so I told her about Envirogal and offered to bring her some samples. I might have gone overboard and brought her a sample or two of *every* product we had. Look, I stand by the product and I love sharing it with friends and neighbors. Since then, I like to bring her fun stuff from the office.

She waves goodbye and I turn to unlock our mailbox. Becca is horrible at checking our mail, so I make it a point to check our box every night when I get home. I pull out a small stack of mail and head home.

It was a long day at work. We are doing some market studies on women's hair care, which Envirogal is considering branching off into. Before we can do that though, hours upon hours of market research, focus groups, and multiple surveys need to take place. Needless to say, I've been working some very long hours over the past couple of weeks. I could use a glass of wine and a good book before passing out for the night. Standing in the elevator, I causally look through the mail. Bill, bill, junk, the latest copy of *The Progressive*, and a letter addressed to me.

The handwriting is sloppy, and I know immediately who it's from. Levi. Turning over the envelope in my hand, I carefully open it. It's a notecard, *"from the desk of **Levi King**"* in gold embossed script. I fight an eyeroll. I open it up and read.

My dearest sister, I wanted to formally remind you that you are required to attend all the previously requested events leading up to my wedding. Since you have not RSVP'd to any of the events, I assume you are trying to figure out a way to get out of them. No can do, little sister. You must face the King family and support your amazingly talented, extremely handsome brother. If I have to be in attendance, so do you. Yours truly, best brother in the world.

I stifle a laugh as I unlock my door and walk inside.

"What's so funny?" Becca is sitting on the couch with her laptop in her lap.

I shut the door and drop the mail on the small console just inside the front door and place my keys in the dish that sits on it. "Oh, just this letter from Levi."

"He sends you letters now? Can't he just text like normal people?"

I sit down next to her and lean back into the comfy cushions. "Apparently, I haven't RSVP'd to any of the upcoming wedding festivities. He was just reminding me that I needed to." I close my eyes and sigh. I love just being home.

"That's right, it's all coming up soon. The wedding is in what, three months?" Becca shuts her computer and slides it onto the end table.

I don't bother opening my eyes, but confirm, "Yes. But the engagement party is next weekend and then a couple weeks after that is the shower, which is a couples event. Barf. Clearly, I'll be at the wedding, so I guess I didn't see a need to RSVP right away. I've had the actual wedding invitation for all of two days. But you know Kitty."

"I'm sorry I'm unable to attend the wedding with you, but I'm already booked at that conference."

I can hear the sadness in her voice. She dislikes my family as much as I do, but she is always my plus one. I need someone to have my back when I have to spend time in the lion's den. I don't know if I mentioned this but Becca is a bartender. Since she comes from money, she's what people lovingly refer to as a socialite. She doesn't have to work. But she has a degree in economics from Columbia. And instead of actually working in that field, she bartenders at a swanky little place called Bar Eros.

"Yeah, yeah. Whatever." I crack a smile, on the brink of falling asleep.

"I just hate that you have to face the vultures alone."

"I won't be alone. Levi will be there."

"Um, he's the groom. He's not going to be able to hang out with you the whole time. He'll be busy."

She has a point. Ugh. Now my excitement level for the wedding events went from a solid three to a point-five.

"You know what you need?" she says.

I lift my eyebrow in question.

"You need a boyfriend. That way you drag him with you to those events and not only will you have someone who has your back, you'll have that same someone to sneak off with when things get boring."

Opening my eyes, I turn and look at her. "Sure, let me get right on that. I'll just go get a boyfriend and on our second or third date tell him I want him to meet my family."

"Ooh, you know what you should do? You should hire some guy to be your fake boyfriend." She tucks her legs up under her and turns toward me. She looks excited.

I sit up, no longer relaxed. "I feel like this came out of nowhere."

"I stumbled upon that old Debra Messing movie today. You know, the one where she hires Dermot Mulroney's character to be her wedding date. But he's a male escort, so it's pretty funny. I forgot how much I loved that movie. Then after that, *Pretty Woman* came on. So … it's been festering in my mind all day."

I chuckle. "Well, two great movies, but I'm not hiring a male escort to take home to my family who already has labeled me the black sheep." I stand and head to my room to get into more comfortable clothing. A pair of leggings and a hoodie have been calling my name all day.

"Oh my god, Emmy. You would only hire an escort if you wanted to have sex with him too. And by the way, *ew*. I think you could find some nice guy— from work maybe—and ask him to do you a favor. Offer him some money for his time. Give him some basic family details and call it a day," she says from the doorway of my room.

I'm standing in my hose and underwear as I hang up my dress. "No way. I don't think I have enough money to offer up to the poor soul I would willingly take to meet my family. Plus, I don't even know what the going rate for a fake boyfriend is these days." I roll my eyes, sitting down to take off my stockings.

"Hmm ... I would say since it's all wedding related, two grand an event."

My eyes bulge. "That's eight thousand, Becca. I'm not made of money."

"Actually ..." she trails off with a smile.

"I don't even know why we are still having this conversation. I'm not hiring some random guy to pretend to be my boyfriend for a few weeks."

She shrugs just as someone knocks at our front door.

I look at her quizzically and she turns away from me. "Must be maintenance to fix our garbage disposal. I'll let him in."

I stand from my bed and shut my door. Thank you, Becca, for leaving my door wide open to let some guy into our apartment while I'm standing here in my bra.

Behind my now closed door, their voices are now muted. I finish dressing and pick up my phone just as it rings. It's Levi.

"Hey! I got your note today. How thoughtful of you." I smile in greeting.

"I just needed to make sure you were coming to the wedding." He chuckles, but I can tell he's just playing.

"I don't know, I might be busy. I might need to wash my hair."

"Ha, ha. Look, Kitty is driving me mad. She keeps bitching about how you've not RSVP'd yet."

"I got the invitation in the mail two days ago, Levi."

"I can hear the eyeroll, Ems." He knows me too well.

"Side note, when is Kitty not bitching about me?" I offer, because the answer is all the time.

"True story."

"The end."

"I should probably warn you now, I just got word that she's expecting you to come alone, and she's inviting Craig. She's seating you together. So, you might want to bring a plus one."

"Why?" I moan and throw myself onto my bed, very dramatic-like. It would be GIF worthy for sure.

"Don't shoot the messenger. Hey, I have another call I've got to take."

"Okay, later."

"Bye, Ems."

The line goes dead.

Shit.

In addition to dealing with my family, the last thing I need is having to put up with Craig, my fucking ex-boyfriend. His family and mine go way back. When we were kids, we got along pretty well, then we dated for a few years in college. We ended it for few reasons. One, he fully expected me to become his wife, to put my brand-new diploma in a cabinet somewhere and tend to his beck and call. And two, I suspected that he was not being faithful. Plus, I really wasn't that into him. I didn't like him enough to put my career and dreams in a drawer and be the wife of a cheating, high-powered douche-lord.

Damn Kitty. She knows he's a dick. She's doing it to punish me, that's for sure. If only I *did* have a boyfriend. But I've been so focused on my career, I haven't really had time. I have dated a little, but there's been nothing serious.

Mentally, I start to run through a list of single men I know who might be interested in being my date. There's Seth, from the marketing department. He's nice. Single. But he's also kind of my direct report. Hmmm. Mark from accounting, he's nice. But I think he is dating Janice from sales. I'm going to have to inquire about that tomorrow. I'm racking my brain for more men, when my phone beeps with a text.

Bex: I've just had the most brilliant idea ever.

Me: Oh, yay. Can't wait to hear it.

Me: Why are you texting me?

The three bouncing dots show up on the screen while she types. I'm tempted to just get up and open my door to talk to her. But just then a picture comes through. It's from our kitchen. Front and center is Jake the maintenance man, bending over our sink. He's wearing a heather gray T-shirt, highlighting his muscular back. The snug-fit jeans, I suspect would hang low on his waist if it weren't for his belt.

My god, that man is sexy.

Me: Are you creeping on him?
Bex: I'm allowed to take pictures of my kitchen whenever I want.
Me: So, what's your brilliant idea?
Bex: Hire him as your fake boyfriend.

No way. I couldn't.

No, I couldn't ask Jake. I don't even know him. I mean, I see him around the building. He's worked here for a few years. Everyone loves him. He seems like a nice guy. He would probably think I'm a crazy woman if I just ask him to pretend to be my date.

There's no way I can ask him.

No way would he say yes.

ake

I'M ALMOST positive she just took a picture of me. The pretty blonde that lives here has always been friendly. She's flirted a time or two, but it seemed harmless. She seems like the kind of woman who would get bored easily. Out of the corner of my eye, I can see her body angled toward me, and her phone is where I can see it. Also directed at me. Which puts her into the creepy, "must-avoid residents" column. The column is growing at an astounding rate.

Thankfully, this maintenance call is legit and isn't some ploy to get me up here alone with her. I know the blonde, Becca, has a roommate, but she must not be here. She's actually never been here at the same time as my past maintenance calls to their unit. Which is kind of a bummer since she's sexy as fuck. But it's for the best. I'd rather appreciate from afar.

They've got a relatively easy fix tonight. A leaky gasket on their garbage disposal. They reported a leak under their sink two days ago, but we've been slammed downstairs with a few higher priority issues in the building. I instructed them to place a large bowl or dish under the unit and avoid using the disposal. They've followed my directions and for that, they will get a gold star. I keep a mental tally of which residents are actually worth a damn. Some people, I swear to you, couldn't follow a simple instruction if their life depended on it.

Thinking about this has me shaking my head to myself. After reattaching the plug to the garbage disposal and dishwasher drain hose, I start to pack up my tool kit.

"Well, this was an easy fix. The gasket was getting pretty old, so I replaced it. You shouldn't have any more leaking."

"Oh, that's great news." Becca is leaning against the end of the couch, like I expected, facing where I was working.

"Em, did you hear that? He said we are easy." She says this right as the room-mate in question enters the living room from what I assume is her bedroom.

I clear my throat. "That's not what I said."

Becca lifts a shoulder but is looking at her roommate.

The brunette must be used to Becca's antics because she just smiles then addresses me. "So, what was the issue?"

"Leaky gasket. It was an easy fix." Now that I'm taking her in, I don't think I could look away if I wanted to. Her dark hair is up on the top of her head in a messy bun. She's wearing a gray Cornell hoodie and black leggings. She's also barefoot. There is something about this low-key look that I'm drawn to. It's like she doesn't care what people think of her. She's going to do what she wants. And clearly, she wants to be dressed for comfort, not first impressions.

"Oh, that's good. I'm glad it wasn't anything worse. I can't imagine having to live without a garbage disposal." She smiles and I can see the laughter in her eyes.

I crack a smile. We stand there for a moment, smiling at each other when Becca speaks.

"Jake, have you ever dated for money?" Her eyes widen and her gaze swings toward Becca as I replay the words back in my mind.

"Excuse me?" My stare hardens on Becca. I'm not sure where this is going. I doubt I will like it.

"Well, Emmy here has a proposition for you." She crosses her arms, looking like she's about to start negotiating a big-money deal.

"I do not." Emmy gasps and I steal a glance at her and can easily see her face redden.

So, this is Emmy. She's damn sexy all dressed up and down, but she's fucking adorable when she's embarrassed. And now I'm curious as to what this proposition is.

The two women seem to have a silent conversation and I ping-pong glances between the two.

Finally, Becca speaks, "Emmy needs a fake boyfriend for some upcoming family events. I happen to think you'd be perfect for the job." She's not even paying attention to Emmy anymore.

"A fake boyfriend," I repeat.

"Roger that." Becca looks serious, but I'm not sure if this isn't just a joke at my or Emmy's expense. The uneasy feeling is pissing me off.

I glare at Becca and then do the same to Emmy. "Are you guys fucking with me right now?"

"Uh—" Emmy stammers her reply, but Becca cuts her off.

"She really needs a date."

"No, I don't. It wouldn't work anyway," Emmy replies. She is wringing her hands. Now I'm just annoyed. I don't have time for this shit. Stupid games of the rich little Upper West Side princesses.

I bend down to grab my toolbox. "I don't have time for this."

"She'll pay you," Becca sings.

"I'm not an escort."

"We are not suggesting that at all." Emmy takes a step toward me.

Becca huffs at Emmy's attempt to placate me. "Think about it as a vacation from your normal, boring life. You get to wine and dine with the fat cats and pretend to be someone you're not. Pocket a shit ton of cash and be on your way. Seems like a no-brainer to me."

I continue to glare at Becca, having no idea what to say. Shaking my head, I walk to the door. I'm not even going to reply to that. Clearly, Emmy isn't going to attempt to dig them both out of the hole they just dug. I get about a step away from the front door when I remember the giant-ass Skee-Ball machine in the corner of their apartment. While I would normally ask if I could play a round or two, I'm feeling vindictive.

"I know for a fact you didn't get that machine approved by management. You're looking at a fucking-hefty fine for having this up here. I should probably report you for it," I threaten, looking over my shoulder at the two socialites.

Becca rolls her eyes. Emmy on the other hand looks panicked.

"I'll pay you ten thousand dollars to be my date and keep your mouth shut about the Skee-Ball machine." The words are out of Emmy's mouth before I get my hand on the doorknob.

I slowly turn and look at her. Did she really just offer me ten grand?

"Four dates. Two thousand each plus an additional two not to mention the machine." She stands her ground.

Oh shit. She's for real with this.

"You don't have to pretend to be anyone you're not. But I don't want to face my family alone. My brother's getting married, and I need someone who's gonna have my back."

I can't believe what I'm hearing right now. She's clearly got issues. "You're fucking insane. Both of you." With that I turn on my heel and leave.

Still mentally chewing on the craziness I was just subjected to, I step out of the elevator. Just then, crazy Sara, from my botched date the other night, walks through the building's entrance.

Shit.

She's looking down at her phone, so I make a beeline for the massive potted plant to the left of the elevators. Normally I wouldn't stoop to this level of ridiculousness, but I don't want to engage in any kind of conversation with her. So, I hide.

I fucking hide from her.

I duck down behind the plant as she walks past. She waits briefly for the elevator doors to open then she steps in. Once I hear them slide shut, I peek through the greenery. She's nowhere in sight, so I stand to my full height. Brushing off my jeans, I shift my gaze around the lobby to make sure no one saw me.

Looks like I'm in the clear.

Phew.

What is it with this building? All of a sudden, I've found myself surrounded by crazy women. First Crazy Sara and now the girls on the fourteenth floor. If the craziness keeps popping up, it might be time I update my resume.

Hours later, when I return to my apartment, I can't stop thinking about Emmy's proposition. There is a slip in my mailbox from the super, letting me know my application for the shower renovation I requested has been denied. My shower is causing some kind of leak. I'm not sure of the damage it's already caused, but I'm worried if it's not addressed sooner rather than later, we could have a major issue on our hands. The unit just under mine may end up with a leak of their own, which then means *their* unit will be at risk for mold and a sunken-in ceiling. The project isn't extremely difficult. It's one I could manage on my own. But it's the cost that could be an issue. We are looking at at least five grand. If I want this fixed, I will have to fix it myself. As in, cover the cost. I've already put so much of my own money into this unit.

I keep taking money from my savings, making my dream of buying my own house on the island seem farther and farther away. I grew up on the island so settling down there someday just makes sense to me.

Damn it, that brown-eyed beauty and her fucking money is looking better and better. I start to contemplate the idea of being her fake boyfriend. I'm for shit not going to pretend to be someone I'm not. And what dude wants to go to a wedding to begin with? There will need to be some kind of bonus tacked on for that kind of date.

Slumping down into my worn leather couch I realize that I'd be a fool to not take this deal. I know I told her she was crazy, but I don't think Emmy is the same level of crazy as Sara. I kind of feel bad for jumping her shit without considering her offer, but what's done is done. The point is, I'm considering it now. Since these dates wouldn't be real, let's call it a business deal, I'm not at risk of compromising my no-dating-the-residents rule.

All right. It's been decided. I'll talk to Emmy tomorrow with a counteroffer.

It looks like I'm about to be the fake boyfriend of some high-society princess.

mmy

THE DAY after my impromptu request of Jake being my fake boyfriend, I find myself in a rather grouchy mood. When he left our apartment last night, Bex lost it and laughed at the whole situation. Me, I was embarrassed. Also, mad. At both Bex, Jake, and even myself. I'm pissed with Bex because this whole debacle could have been avoided if she had kept her trap shut. I'm annoyed with Jake because, well, he's a major asshole—a hot asshole, no doubt—but I'm thinking that the hotter guys are, the more asshole-ish they get.

Mostly, I'm mad at myself for stooping so low I'd ask a near stranger to be my fake boyfriend. I barely have ten grand in my savings account, why I would offer all that up, I don't know.

After leaving work early due to a foul mood, I'm sitting here now, relaxing on the couch. I don't cut out early often, but my work wasn't the grade-A quality it usually is, so I left. Now I'm binge watching Marvel's *Gifted*. Any show with the former Bill Compton is a winner in my book. But I'm always down for a little mutant, *X-Men* action. Fortunately, Bex isn't here to hound me about everything *X-Men*. She asks a lot of questions.

I'm just getting into my third episode when my phone rings. I look down and let out a groan. Craig, my ex. Why is he calling me? It's been nearly two years since I've even seen him. I assumed he lost my number. Well, I had hoped he did. Then again, I should have lost his. Unsure if it's the right decision, I answer the phone.

"Hello?"

"Hey, baby doll. It's Craig."

"Yeah, I know. You're still the only one who calls me baby doll. Which I still hate."

"You're still adorable, I see. So, word on the street is that you're finally ready to settle down."

"Ugh, no. Where did you hear that?"

"I ran into Kitty today. She said you were missing me and invited me to Levi's wedding and pre-wedding affairs."

"Great."

"I'm looking forward to seeing you again," he purrs in that seductive voice he thinks is the secret to him getting laid with. It has the opposite effect on me, it just makes my skin crawl.

"I'm being sarcastic, Craig. I don't know why, but Kitty made all of that up. And I'm annoyed that she would tell you that stuff."

"Right, and Kitty would just lie about something like that. I get it, you're not ready to admit it just yet, so I will take the leap first. I miss you too though, baby doll."

I groan. "Craig, just stop."

"I'm looking forward to rekindling our world-class romance."

I fight a gag, Craig is gross. I know how busy he's been since we broke up, making his way through all the well-known and wannabe socialites. Looks like I will have to play some hardball to get him to back off.

"Look, Craig, I don't know how to say this without sounding like a jerk, I'm not interested. When we broke up, I was serious. We are never getting back together."

He chuckles. He's always had a hard time taking a hint. "Look at you, quoting bad pop songs."

"Taylor Swift is a phenomenal songwriter." I don't know why I feel the need to defend the pop princess, but I do it anyway.

"Whatever you say, Emmy." I can tell by his mocking tone that he's still not hearing me.

"I'm dating someone and I'm happy with where that's going right now."

"Really? Are you really trying that line?" he tests.

"We are very happy, I'm not pulling any *line* with you."

"Nothing can rival your first love. You'll see. All I need is one dance and you'll be swooning in my arms once again."

"I've never swooned for you."

"You keep telling yourself that, baby doll."

"I'm hanging up now." And then I do.

Tossing my phone on the couch next to me, I realize what I just did.

Shit, shit, shitballs.

I really need a boyfriend now. Unfortunately, the engagement party is less than a week away. There isn't enough time.

Just as I'm contemplating what the downfalls of a name change and an escape to Mexico might be, there's a knock at the door. To my surprise, it's Jake.

"I wasn't expecting to see you again." He's without his toolbox, so I know he isn't here on official maintenance business.

"Yeah, tell me about it. Can I come in?"

I should tell him to go away. He was a total jerk to a poor woman in need of his help. Me being the poor woman.

I move and open the door wider to let him in. I get the door closed right as he talks.

"I've thought more about your fake boyfriend scheme. And I'll do it, but I have conditions."

"Um, excuse me, but it's not a scheme."

"Whatever. Are you still in need of my help or not?" He folds his arms across his chest. I can't help noticing the thick, corded muscles of his biceps and —*oh, those forearms.* I mentally check to make sure I'm not drooling.

"Yes, I'm still in need of a date." I mirror his pose, I'm not about to let him come in here and try to intimidate me.

"All right, first condition. You pay me fifteen grand. You're asking me to go to a fucking wedding." I try to hide the discomfort that fills me at his request. I don't have fifteen thousand. He keeps going, "Second condition is that you buy me whatever clothes and shit I'll need to wear to these events. I live in jeans, sneakers, and T-shirts. So, if you want me to play the part, pay for it. My third and final condition, no sex. I'm not a man whore and I don't fuck residents."

Damn, he's a cocky son of a bitch. His stunted view toward the rich and well, me, is stupid-annoying. Yet, his give-no-fucks attitude is kind of hot. I'm struggling between being turned on and pissed. Maybe each emotion is feeding the other.

I let the anger emotion take over. "I have my own condition." I jut my hip out a bit, showing him that I mean business.

"Yeah? And what's that?" He smiles at my indignation.

"Don't ever call me crazy or insane again."

"Really? That's your condition?" He thinks this is a joke.

"Yes. I'm completely sane. Every decision I make has been carefully made and made in my best interest. I don't appreciate people who don't understand me and my decisions blowing me off by calling me crazy. Don't do it again." I'm dead serious when I say I'm so sick and tired of people calling me that. If I had a quarter for every time someone called me crazy when I walked away from my family's money, I would be a self-made millionaire by now for sure.

"Why do people call you crazy? Is there something I need to know about?" he asks me, but I can tell it won't sway his decision.

"I'm not interested in getting into it with you."

"Fine, whatever. So, what will it be? Fake boyfriend or not?"

Ugh, I don't have fifteen grand, but I do have a bonus coming up next month. Maybe it will be enough to cover. I will have to save more. Becca will understand that I can't go out to eat as much. I'll charge the new clothes to my credit card. It's got a substantial limit, one I never reach. You'd think a person growing up with a silver spoon in their mouth would be prone to poor money management when left to do it on their own, but no, not me. I'm on top of my shit. I hear my phone text tone from the couch and remember my call with Craig. I have no choice.

"Deal." I thrust my hand out for a shake.

He seems a little relieved himself, but still puts off his don't-mess-with-me vibe as he takes my hand in his. "Deal," he agrees, as he should since I didn't bother negotiating his terms.

I drop his hand and move to sit back down on the couch. I glance at my phone and see a text from Levi asking why Craig thinks I have a boyfriend. Wow shit travels fast. I ignore him for now.

"So, I'll need dates and times. I've got a lot of personal time banked up, plus just about everybody on the team owes me more than one favor. But as much notice as possible would be best."

I gesture to the lounge chair next to me. He sits. Finally, he isn't acting like such a tool.

"Yeah, I have all the dates already. The engagement party is first up, it's next week, actually." I brace myself as I know it's short notice, but Jake doesn't react. "Then a couple weeks later, the shower, it's a couples thing. But then we have a little break before the rehearsal and wedding. If you give me your number, I can text all this info to you. Or I can create a calendar invite."

"An invite works. I'll still give you my number though. So, this wedding, are you in it? Like, am I going to have to fend for myself at all?" He doesn't sound annoyed, more like he wants to be able to prepare for any scenario.

I snort. Ladylike, I know. "Oh, no. I didn't make the cut. My sister-in-law to-be and I do not get along."

He eyes me.

"Isn't it normal for siblings to be part of the wedding party?"

I smile, he's not wrong.

"No, you're right but … well, Darcy, she doesn't really care about tradition. While I love my brother dearly, he just does what she says." I don't share with Jake that Levi and I had a long talk about it after Darcy announced her wedding party. Levi wanted to make sure I was okay with it but also thought maybe it was letting me off the hook since I didn't want to be part of that life anymore. While I'm sad I don't get to be a true part of his big day, I appreciate his reasoning. And I will try to enjoy it like everyone else. Plus, I can't stand Darcy, if he were marrying someone I actually liked, I'd feel differently for sure.

"So, I need clothes. I'll take your lead on what I'm expected to wear to these things. When do you want to take care of that?"

"Are you free Saturday? I've got all day open, so we can work around your schedule," I offer.

"I have to clock in at three, so how about that morning? Where will we be shopping? Barneys? Bloomingdale's? Saks?"

I try not to cringe at the thought of the cost per outfit at those stores. I do almost all my shopping at Century 21, a discounted name-brand store. I haven't shopped with a personal stylist since college. I don't know why I feel compelled to keep Jake thinking I'm some high-society princess. So, I bite the bullet.

"We can meet up at Bloomingdale's. Ten sharp, men's department." A wave of disgust washes over me due to my lie of omission. So, I stand. It's time for him to leave. He takes the hint and stands as well.

"I've got one more question. Why does someone like you need a fake boyfriend anyway?"

I bristle at the comment. "What do you mean, someone like me?"

He looks me up and down and moves his hand along with the perusal. "You, you're young and attractive, you seem put together."

I relax at his assessment.

"Plus, isn't there some kind of rich fuck dating pool? Silver spoons stick together, right?"

Now I want to throat punch him. I straighten my shoulders, holding my head up high when I reply.

"It's none of your business. We've all got issues and I would appreciate it if you'd be a little less judgy. I'm not judging you about why you so badly need fifteen grand, so maybe you could show the same respect toward me."

His eyebrows lift as he nods. "Fair enough, I'll keep the judging to a minimum, or at least to myself."

I roll my eyes and show him to the door. It isn't until he's long gone that I realize I never got his number. That's fine. I'll get it Saturday after I sell an arm and a leg to cover his new clothes.

CHAPTER 8

ake

STANDING outside the massive building that is Bloomingdale's, I have to take a few breaths before I go in. Never in my life did I ever expect to step foot in this department store. Seeing it portrayed enough through movies and TV, I know I'm not part of the clientele they cater to. No, I'm sure I couldn't even afford a simple pocket square. Ripping the Band-Aid off, I head inside.

Finding the men's department is easy enough. Scanning the area for Emmy, I loiter as close to the elevators as I can when I realize she isn't here yet. I gently run my thumb and forefinger over the lapel of a dark gray blazer. The buttery-soft fabric is a definite selling point. If I were a businessman, I'd buy several. I slide my hand up and over the shoulder and down the sleeve of the blazer where I find the price tag. Flipping it over in my hand I try not to let my jaw fall to the floor when I see it's nearly six hundred dollars. I drop the sleeve like a hot potato and take a step away from the rack.

Shit, rich people clothes are expensive. If just a blazer costs that much money, how much will an entire outfit cost? A slight, very tiny spark of guilt pricks at me when I realize I requested Emmy buy me enough outfits to cover all four dates. What's she going to spend here today? Two grand at least? But the feeling flees as soon as I remember that two grand for a few outfits is nothing for her.

"Jake! Hey, sorry I'm late." Emmy walks up and stands next to me.

She's freaking gorgeous. She's wearing a bright yellow dress with a denim jacket over it, the sleeves rolled up to her elbows. A wide brown belt sits high on her waist. The bottom of her dress is covered in flowers and her heels add a couple inches to her height, bringing the top of her head to my chin. She's smiling at me as my eyes wander back to her face. Her hair is down today, barely past her shoulders and slightly curly, and I can't help but wonder how soft it would feel with my face buried in her neck.

Damn, man. Get it together.

"Hey. I just got here myself."

"Oh, good. Well, let's get this over with." She eyes the blazer I was looking at. Maybe I'm imagining it, but did she just cringe? Just as I'm about to ask, we are joined by a sales associate.

"Good morning, my name is Sasha. Is there anything I can help you with today?" I look to Emmy for an answer and she's on it.

"Yes. We've got some pre-wedding events to attend and ..."

The sales lady cuts in, "Say no more. I'm on it. What kind of events are we talking about?"

"An engagement party and shower."

"Perfect. What are your sizes, sweetie, and I'll go pull some outfits that I think would look fabulous on you." She directs her question at me. I'm a little stunned but manage to mumble my answer. She scurries off in the direction she came from.

Next to me, Emmy chuckles and tugs my arm. "This is what she does. She works on commission. I don't know the first thing about men's clothes, so let's see what she finds and then we can go from there. Until then, let's get you a dressing room."

I follow her, weaving through racks and shelves of expensive-as-shit clothes.

No sooner do we find the dressing rooms, Sasha floats in with her arms full of clothes. "Here, let me get you started." She veers into a tiny room and makes quick work of organizing what she picked out. Which is freaky fast if you ask me. Emmy doesn't seem bothered by it.

"There you go, hon. I'll be back with more. Let me know if you need any other sizes or colors." And in a blink of an eye, she's gone again.

I stand there, a little overwhelmed.

"Hey, Jake, you all right?"

I turn my head toward her and find her trying not to laugh. "I'm fine."

"You look like you have no idea what to do. Have you ever been clothes shopping before?" She's joking around, but I glare anyway.

"Why don't you just go in there, try the outfits she picked out, then come out here and let me see it?"

Grumbling, I turn and walk into the dressing room. I slide the thick curtain closed and clip it to the waiting hook, creating a makeshift wall of privacy.

Surveying the clothes, I groan. I can tell by just looking at the selection I will hate it all.

"Some clothes look better on a person than on the hanger. Give it all a chance." Stifling a groan, I take her advice and start on the first outfit. I hear Emmy move closer to the dressing room, the quiet of the fitting area is almost earie. There is no one else around and she starts to tell me more about herself. She tells me about her job and how she loves it, even though it causes some contention between her and her father since it's technically a competing company. She also shares more about her brother, the one getting married. She seems a little sad when she explains that while they are close, they don't see each other often, despite living in the same city. I can't help but feel there is something she isn't sharing with me. But I remind myself that I'm still a stranger, I don't expect her entire life story. Least of all, not over clothes shopping.

After what feels like hours later, and despite pleasant conversation with a beautiful woman, I'm fucking grumpy. In reality, I know it hasn't been hours. More like forty-five minutes, but Sasha keeps bringing shit that is, well ... shit. It's all bad. It's all been crazy patterns, crazy fabric, or colors I can't even pronounce.

While I've been in my own personal hell trying on hideous outfit after hideous outfit, Emmy seems to have been enjoying my discomfort. We've developed a routine. When I come out of the dressing room, one of two things happen: she either pretends to contemplate the outfit like it might be the best thing she's seen yet, or she bursts out laughing.

I've just taken off the latest disaster when I see Sasha's most recent attempt to find the best style for me.

"Oh hell no."

"Whatever it is, please try it on, Jake," Emmy begs, laughing from the sitting area in the middle of the dressing room area.

This whole thing has been easy for her. She's sitting on a plush, white leather couch enjoying the show.

"No. I've had enough."

"Please, it could be the one." She's pleading with me now. I don't know why I even bother, but I do. Standing there in my socks and briefs, I take in the outfit. The matching plaid suit pants and jacket looks like someone lifted it straight from Sherlock Holmes' wardrobe. I shake my head and grumble as I step into the pants and pull the shirt on. And that's when I decide I can't take any more of this.

"I'm done. This isn't working."

"Let me see, Jake."

"No, I look ridiculous."

"Come on, Jake. Let me see. I won't laugh." She sounds closer now, no longer sitting on the couch.

"No."

"It probably looks better than you think." Now she sounds annoyed.

"No one will ever see me like this." I'm staring at myself in the mirror wondering how I even got to this moment when I see the curtain move.

"Jake, let me see." Then I see her fingers wrap around the curtain. Turning, I grab her hand. She yelps as I pull her into the tiny dressing room with me.

Once she's in, I snap the curtain shut behind her.

She stands there staring at me. I let her get her fill. She presses her lips together as she takes me in. Her eyes twitch. When she can't hold it in anymore, she bursts out laughing. "Oh my god. You look like Doctor Who." More laughing.

I cross my arms and roll my eyes.

"That's it. I'm cutting you off. You don't get to see what I'm working with anymore."

She calms her laughter and shakes her head. "Nope. You have to show me. I'll stay in here if I have to." She mimics my pose and looks adorably annoying being all bossy.

"And I said no," I push back.

"If I'm paying for this shit, I'm sure as hell going to approve of what I'm buying." And just like that, I'm fucking turned on. She's no longer laughing, and her annoyance is palpable.

I lower my tone and take a few steps toward her. "Then I guess you won't be buying shit today, babe."

Her arms drop to her sides and she takes a step back, bumping into the wall.

"I've tried on more than two dozen outfits and I'm spent. I'm hungry, I'm annoyed, and I'm tired of dressing up in clown clothes." I move in closer to her. There isn't much more space between us.

She straightens her shoulders and pushes her hair away from her face. She looks me in the eyes as she says it, but her eyes drop to my mouth. "We have to find something today, or our deal is over and no money for you."

"Then I guess you won't have a fake boyfriend." Now that I'm so damn close to her, I can't help lifting my hand to snag a wayward strand of her hair. Grasping it between my fingers, I can confirm that it's as soft as I imagined earlier. I twist it around my finger, watching the movement. I turn my attention back to her and find she is watching as well. She lifts her eyes and looks into mine, then back down to my lips. She bites her bottom lip and I lean in. I want to bite that lip and taste it for myself. I'm so close I can feel her breath mix with my own.

"Jake, Emmy? Are you in there? I have more outfits," Sasha sings. She has perfect timing because I take one last glance at Emmy's lips, drop her hair, and back away.

Emmy clears her throat, avoids eye contact and pushes out of the dressing room.

"You know what, Sasha, these outfits just aren't working. Why don't we go simple? I already have my outfits picked out, why don't we try to coordinate?" Emmy suggests.

Damn, that was a close one. I don't know what came over me, but I almost kissed Emmy. There can be none of that. My time with her is business, not pleasure.

"Oh, I can't believe I never asked you what you were wearing! That's a wonderful idea." Sasha plays off the fact that we were just in the dressing room together like it isn't a big deal. I adjust myself in my pants then remember I'm wearing a fucking Sherlock Holmes costume.

I don't know whether to be pissed with Emmy or not. Once she told Sasha what she was wearing, it took another twenty minutes, and I had three outfits boxed up and ready to be paid for. Had she started this shopping experience with that, we would have been done in no time.

Emmy seems quiet as she pulls out her credit card. I expect it to be black, or gold—don't the rich and famous get the good, prestigious cards? But no, hers is green, and looks like just a regular bank card. I don't think I can handle knowing the final price of the trip, so I turn away and study a display of sunglasses.

While I'm glad we are done shopping, I'm not ready to say goodbye to her yet. Plus, I need to get a read on her mood change. Did the almost kiss piss her off? She seemed fine during the last leg of our outfit adventure.

She grabs the bags off the counter and turns to me. "Here you go, three new outfits. I don't have my dress for the wedding yet, but we have time to get you something else. Like after the fifth of the month."

I quirk my head at the last comment but take the clothes. "So, you want to get lunch?"

She shrugs. "I could eat."

"I was thinking you should probably give me the low-down on what I need to know for this engagement party."

She chews on the inside of her lip. "Yeah, that's a good idea."

"Is there any place you want to eat near here?" I look over to her as we exit the building. It's sunny out so she pulls out a pair of big-rimmed sunglasses. Somehow, they match her outfit perfectly.

I look away and squint, wishing I'd brought my own pair.

"Actually, there is this little cafe a couple blocks away. Can we go there?" I plan on picking up the bill, I am a gentleman, but I'm hoping like hell this "little" cafe will not be as outrageously priced as I expect.

Idle chitchat gets us through the relatively short walk to the cafe. We walk right in and get a seat. I pick up the menu and find lots of soups, salads, and sandwiches. I notice the pricing isn't so bad. The salads must be their specialty because they are the most overpriced items on the menu. I always find it interesting what someone orders on a first date. Of course, this isn't a date, but it's the first meal we've shared. I think what a person orders says a lot about them. Girls that order a plain-Jane salad then claim they are nervous or aren't very hungry annoy the shit out of me. I shared my theory with a friend of mine a few years back and she agreed wholeheartedly. She'd had a first date in a nice restaurant and the tool ordered a half-and-half plate of bone-in wings and BBQ ribs. She said he proceeded to tuck a napkin into his collar and then licked his fingers clean when he was done. See what I mean? Is that really first-date material? Nope.

But I can't help but smile when Emmy orders a simple grilled cheese and a bowl of tomato soup. I order the chicken club and side of the house-made chips. She catches my smile and shrugs a shoulder.

"Grilled Cheese? Really?" I tease.

"What? Don't make fun. I have a serious obsession with them." She picks up the Ball jar full of water and takes a sip.

"How old are you?" I chuckle.

"Twenty-eight. And I'll be ninety before I ever give up my love of hot, melty cheese, sandwiched between two perfectly grilled pieces of bread."

"We came here specifically for the grilled cheese, didn't we?"

Her shoulder lifts causally. "It's possible."

I laugh again. "I happen to make a mean grilled cheese. You'd be so lucky to partake in its amazingness someday."

"I'm sure. So where did this obsession come from?" I doubt this is knowledge I truly need to know to pass as her boyfriend, but I'm intrigued.

Leaning back in her chair, she sweeps a hand in front of her, already brushing off the story. "My nanny growing up made them for me all the time. We would spend hours experimenting with different cheeses, coming up with the best combinations. Finding the perfect bread and whether or not it's best to butter both sides of the bread." She leans in. "Hint: it is."

"Okay, so what is it?" Her eyebrow cocks at my question. "What ingredients make up the best grilled cheese?"

She smirks. "Wouldn't you like to know?" God damn she's adorable.

A guffaw from deep in my belly causes us both to just sit there laughing and smiling at each other. The service here is quick because, moments later, our plates are carefully set down in front of us. Sure enough, her sandwich looks pretty spectacular.

She wastes no time taking a bite. Her moan of ecstasy over a damn grilled cheese causes me to squirm in my seat. Then, she catches me off guard by stretching out her arm offering me a bit of the very food that she just took a bite of.

"Here, you have to try it."

I don't reply but take the triangle from her and take a bite of my own.

Now I understand the moaning. I don't think I've ever had a grilled cheese taste so dang good before.

"Good, right? Now you're going to crave grilled cheese for at least the next week or two."

I hand it back to her and dig into my own sandwich. I refuse to dwell on the fact that she had no issues sharing food with me. We don't know each other, yet she felt comfortable enough for such an intimate gesture.

Which brings me back to why we are here. "So, tell me more about you. What do I need to know?"

Nodding her head, she launches into basic information about her family and some people we will meet at the engagement party in a couple days.

Hours later when I start my shift at Madison, I realize just how much fun I had today with Emmy. Maybe after all this is said and done, we can be friends. A friend I wouldn't mind kissing, but a friend nonetheless.

CHAPTER 9

mmy

"EMMY, Jake's going to be here in like twenty minutes, and you have yet to come out here. I need to check you out, darling." Becca knocks on my door and has been pestering me all evening since I started getting ready. She's seen my dress, but she wasn't with me when I bought it months ago.

"I'm almost done. Hold your horses." I finish applying my nude lip gloss. I like to keep my makeup simple. I opted for a smoky brown on my eyelids to make my deep brown eyes pop. In addition to my gloss, my makeup isn't noticeable, and I prefer it that way. Opening my bedroom door, I'm face-to-face with Becca.

She whistles. "Holy shiitake mushrooms, Em. You look fucking sexy as hell."

I turn around so she can get a look at the back, which is my favorite part of the dress.

"Oh my god. I'm dead," she exclaims. I laugh.

I'm wearing a Kelly green dress that hangs just past my knees. The green beading that winds randomly over the front of the bodice, continues through the lace back that cuts into a deep v, which dips down to the waist of the dress where the skirt starts. Wearing a bra with this dress is pretty much impossible, so I've got my breasts taped into the bodice. Thankfully, the dress isn't cut low in the front. I won't have to live in fear of one of the girls popping out.

The dress is simple elegance, it really has a vintage look to it. I got it for a steal for less than two hundred. It's more than what I normally like paying for an outfit, but when I saw it in the store, I knew it was one of a kind. And bonus, it was in my size. It was fate that this dress and I became one. I wear my hair up in a fancy chignon, to show off the epic backing. The green lace with beading really is to die for.

"I know, I about died when I saw it in the store," I tell her, and then walk over to the couch to start shoving my essentials into a small clutch.

"Jake will be fighting a woody all night for sure."

I turn around and glare at her. "This isn't for Jake, and I doubt it."

"Right." She draws out the word as she walks over and sits down on the couch.

"Don't give me that. If I'm going to face my family, I want to look as confident as I feel. This dress does it for me."

"So, you're not nervous for tonight?" She bites her lip, studying me.

"Hell yes, I'm nervous. One can be confident and nervous at the same time, for sure."

"What are you most worried about? Your family, dealing with Cringey Craig, or that everyone will see through your relationship"—she air-quotes that last word—"with Jake?"

I want to tell her all of it plus the tiny bit about being with Jake again. I haven't seen him since our shopping trip and lunch. I have not mentioned what almost happened between us in the dressing room to Becca. She'd have too much of a field day with that.

I'm not necessarily worried about being with him, more like I'm worried this new tension between us in the Bloomingdale's will grow, and while I'm not completely against it, I haven't completely been truthful with him regarding my situation. Not to mention his rule of not sleeping with residents. I'm not moving anytime soon, and he loves his job here.

I settle on, "All the above."

"Well, Craig will take one look at you and Jake and back off. Jake's got at least fifty pounds on that scrawny ass. As for your parents, just keep your inter-actions with them to a minimum. That way they can't start questioning you about your relationship."

She makes valid points.

"I guess I'm worried about them being rude to him. I know I told him he didn't have to pretend to be anyone else, but I don't want to give them ammuni-tion to make him feel bad about himself."

"Do you care that he's a maintenance man?"

"Of course not!" I'm a little offended by her question. "I couldn't care less about what he does. He could be a trash man for all I care." Granted, if he were a high-powered businessman, we probably would have not been in the same place at the same time and this little arrangement wouldn't be happening.

She gives me this knowing smirk and raises her hands in submission. "Fair enough, just asking."

Just then, there is a knock on the door. Which means it must be Jake.

I move to the door and open it. While I saw all the outfits, we bought the other day, seeing him now, ready for our pseudo-date takes my breath away. Standing in the doorway, his hands in his pockets, he's swoon worthy. He's wearing a deep navy-blue suit jacket with matching trousers. He decided against the tie, making the white button-up even more pronounced. His walnut leather belt ended up matching the pair of brown Oxfords perfectly.

"Wow, Emmy, you look fantastic." He clears his throat.

"Not so bad yourself, Jake. This outfit is simply … you." I smile, and it's the truth. While I like the normally rugged look of Jake Harper, this dressed-up version is just as spectacular.

"Thank you. I had an excellent stylist." His smile is warm, and it seems like we could actually pass as friends, so making people believe we are more should be easy.

"Well, don't you two just look stunning together. Cringey Craig isn't going to know what hit him. Em, you never looked this good on his arm. Mostly because he looked like a twat ninety-five percent of the time."

I roll my eyes but can't help smiling. She always hated Craig. Isn't it obvious judging by her nickname for him?

When I look back at Jake, he's glaring at her.

"Are you ready?" he grumbles.

"Yes! See ya, Bex." I wave to her as I close the door behind me.

Jake is still glaring and all bristly when we get to the elevator. He pushes the lobby button then turns to me. "Who's Craig?"

"Oh, just my ex. Nothing to worry about." I wave him off.

"You didn't say anything about making an ex jealous. That was not part of the deal. I'm not going to be part of a lovers' quarrel." His body is angled toward me and he looks mad with a mix of disappointed.

My shoulders sag at his words and I let out a sigh. "Craig and I broke up years ago. I broke up with him. My heart wasn't in it. His parents are old family friends of mine. They set us up years ago. When I found out that he had been invited to all these wedding parties, I realized that he and my parents would be relentless in their attempts at getting us back together. That's what created my need for having a plus one. I'm not interested *at all* in Craig, he actually drives me nuts. Bex's nickname for him is legit. He's cringeworthy. Some of the shit that comes out of his mouth is just ..." I shake my head. "I just can't deal with him."

Thankfully, I can tell Jake believes me because his anger melts away from his body during my explanation, but he still sports a hefty scowl.

"So, do you think you can replace that scowl with a smile? You look so much hotter with the smile." I give him my own smile and tilt my head to the side, trying to get any kind of reaction.

His eyebrow twitches and he shifts his lips to the side. Then the tiniest little smile breaks through.

"You think I'm hot?"

"Duh, I wouldn't have asked you to be my fake boyfriend if I didn't. It was the number one requirement."

"Ah, well clearly I made the grade." He plays along, and for that I'm grateful. The last thing I need is to take a grouchy boyfriend, fake or not, into the lion's den with me.

By the time we get to the NoMad Hotel Rooftop, Jake's back to his normal, easygoing self. The one I got to know at lunch the other day. He also exudes confidence because he isn't putting off any kind of vibe that he's anxious. Unlike him, it's clear that I'm a nervous Nellie. If he's uneasy about being at a swanky venue in an upscale part of town, he doesn't show it at all. If anything, he seems to fit in perfectly. Which, I guess is what we were going for with the clothes makeover.

Standing in the elevator taking us up to The Rooftop, the grill and bar my parents rented out for the engagement party tonight, I shift my weight from one hip to the other and I can't seem to keep still.

His hand covers mine, preventing me from twisting them together. "Stop fidgeting. You're fine. We are going to rock this."

"I know, it's just that I get some anxiety when it comes to being around my parents." At lunch, I told him that I didn't have a great relationship with my father and stepmother, instead of the truth, which is that it's much more of a *nonexistent* relationship. I told him that they are just very narrow-minded and hard to please. There's always a possibility that they bring up my self-proclaimed exile, if they do, I'll deal with it. But truthfully, I don't owe him an explanation. This thing between us isn't a real relationship. If it were, then absolutely, honesty is key.

"I get it. But you've got me. I'm here for a reason, Emmy, so it's all good." He's smiling at me, making me feel all tingly, and when the elevator pings our arrival, I realize I'm smiling back and there's definitely something flowing between the two of us.

I've never been to the NoMad Hotel's Rooftop, but upon seeing it for the first time I can tell why my parents picked it. It's everything you would expect from a traditional high-society venue for a party like this. There are several high-top tables set up near the bar area. The granite bar top and white cloth-draped tables only allow seating for around forty people. There are more like sixty here though, but since the terrace provides more lounge-like seating and a dance floor, there's standing room for nearly a hundred. There isn't a DJ, but music is playing, and some attendees are even dancing.

Jake lets out a low whistle as we pause and take in the place. I nod in agreement.

"Swanky much?" I mumble.

He chuckles.

I scan the area for the key players. My father, Kitty, Craig, and Levi. Hoping to find my brother first, I catch the eye of Kitty instead.

I take a deep breath. "Incoming."

Jake reaches over and grabs my hand. "Bring it on."

ake

A TALL, older woman walks toward us. From far away, she looks almost regal, but as she gets closer, I can tell that this is a woman who puts a lot of effort into her appearance in order to make herself look superior. With Emmy's warning, I'm guessing this is her stepmother. I squeeze Emmy's hand to show my support right as the woman stops in front of us.

I don't know Emmy well, but I can feel the shift in the air around her. It surprises me a bit that I can sense this change, but even more so that I don't much like that she's feeling stressed. There is a part of me—a very *small* part— that feels the need to protect her.

"Emerson." She leans in and air kisses Emmy's cheeks. "I'm glad you could make it, even if a bit late." I fight off my desire to make a show of looking at my watch and pointing out that we arrived right on time. There's also something about the way she says "Emerson" that I don't like. Emmy told me that she's always gone by Emmy, so I get the feeling that Kitty's use of her full name is a dig.

"Kitty," is all Emmy says in reply.

I officially have her attention. Just as expected, she looks down her nose at me. I might have imagined the flare of her nostrils. But it makes me feel as if she can smell the lack of wealth on me.

"Are you going to introduce me?" She holds out her elegant hand. Not for a shake, but the way rich bitches do when they want you to kiss the back of their hand. Like she's a fucking queen or something.

"This is my boyfriend, Jake Harper," Emmy tells her, and I swallow my pride and lean forward to take her hand.

"Mrs. King. It's nice to meet you."

"I'm sure you haven't heard anything good, but I have to admit, I've heard absolutely nothing about you." God, she is snooty.

"That's alright. I actually haven't heard anything about you either," I tell her.

Her eyes narrow but she plays it off. I sneak a glance at Emmy, and she doesn't seem irritated at my jab at all. Good.

"So, I take it this thing is new?" Kitty brushes her hand dismissively between the two of us.

"Yes," is all Emmy replies.

"Good. Well, Craig is around here somewhere. I know he is very eager to see you, Emerson." Just like that she's dismissed me.

Emmy leans into me a bit. "Ah, well good for Craig. Like I told him last week, the feeling isn't mutual. Plus, I'm with Jake."

I turn my head slightly and press a kiss to her temple. Kitty studies the gesture before looking away, nodding, and waving to someone nearby. No longer making eye contact with Emmy, she delivers a blow.

"Whatever you say, Emmy. Whatever you think this is between the two of you, won't last. Craig is the real deal and you know it. Stay out of trouble." At that, she turns and walks away.

Emmy lets out a sigh of relief and sags slightly into me. "One down, two more to go."

"That woman is vile. Was that interaction better or worse than you were expecting?" I start to drag her toward the bar. If I'm going to make it through the rest of tonight dealing with that kind of shit, I need a drink. A strong one at that.

"That was actually about on par."

"Do you think your dad is going to be worse? And who's number three? I thought you said Levi is Team Emmy." She chuckles at that.

"Levi isn't number three. His horrid bride-to-be is. We went to school together. I'm pretty sure her one goal in life is to be cast on *The Real Housewives of New York City* someday. Marrying Levi gets her pretty darn close to that goal because of who he is and how much he's worth."

"So, she's going to be a breath of fresh air?"

At that, she laughs, which makes me smile, because I finally get why she didn't want to do this alone.

"What about your dad? Is he going to be like Kitty?" I hand her a glass of house wine. I sip my Manhattan and direct her toward an empty table.

"Hard to say. He will probably be less rude to you, but more judgmental of me. But who knows?"

We sip our drinks and chat about our surroundings. This place is a lot swankier than my normal haunts. It clearly carters to the upper class, but I find myself relaxed here for the most part. I'm not itching to get out. I doubt I'll ever find myself wanting to come back, but I'm not turned off by the atmosphere, a feeling I attribute to my being comfortable with Emmy. I try not to read too much into that feeling. I'm not nor will I ever be someone who frequents a place like this.

She shares little stories about several of the attendees. She points out a woman chatting with her soon-to-be sister-in-law across the room.

"See that woman over there?" She tips her head to the side.

"Yeah, what about her?"

She nods, starting off at the woman. "She used to be one of my closest friends."

"What happened?"

"A couple Christmases ago, I bought her this beautiful vase, she loves getting flowers, has them all over her house. Well, I picked up the vase on sale at this nice vintage boutique, it had her name all over it. You know, one of those gifts you see and just know you have to buy it for that person? Anyway, I kid you not, she took one look at the vase, scrunched her nose, and pushed it to the side." She takes a drink, but she looks amused more than hurt. I'm surprised that there doesn't seem to be an upset or spiteful tone in her voice.

"You mean she wasn't thankful for the gift?" I lean back in my seat, a little surprised that I'm feeling defensive of Emmy's feelings. Not that she's having any kind of feelings I should be defensive over, but I digress.

"That's exactly what I mean. She got mad at me. She was insulted that I gave her trash." She air quotes the last word. Then her smile disappears, she twists her lips to the side, finally showing disdain. "That was the last time we spoke."

"Wow. I don't know what to say, other than good riddance."

She smiles ruefully, bringing the straw of her drink to her lips but adds, "to bad trash."

In that moment my heart thumps inside my chest. Maybe Emmy really isn't like these people surrounding us.

She proceeds to fill me in on who certain people are. She seems to know everyone, so I'm surprised that no one comes to talk to us. It isn't until we are about ready for a second round of drinks when her father finds us. While he doesn't look as warm and inviting as I would expect a father to look, he doesn't look as rigid as his wife. He has Emmy's dark hair, but it has a generous sprinkling of salt through it. He's tall and seems to be in decent shape. His mustache matches his hair—more salt—and I can tell he keeps it well-groomed. I'm personally not a fan of the 'staches, they can get out of hand and make most men look like tools. That's my opinion though.

"Emmy, it's nice to see you," her dad greets.

I let out a breath when he walks right up to her and pulls her into a fatherly hug. She accepts the hug, and I can feel a sense of lingering from both of them, almost like they don't want it to end—as if the peace between them in this moment is about to be lost. When the hug is over, she smiles at him with affection. It takes him a nanosecond to zone in on me.

"I'm Joseph King, Emmy's father. You are?" He holds out his hand and I shake it.

"I'm Jake Harper, Emmy's boyfriend." I'm cool as a cucumber, folks. I wouldn't normally set out to piss off the father of my girlfriend, but I'm not going to let him push me around. Especially since this isn't the real deal.

"Hmm. I see. Well, I don't think anyone knew you were bringing a date." He looks around. "I was just talking to Craig, and I—well, we—were under the impression that the two of you were mending things."

"I told Levi and Craig last week I was bringing a date, Dad. My boyfriend, to use the exact term." She is all confident and it's turning me on. One thing that I'm realizing about Emmy King is that she might be a bundle of nerves on the inside, but when it matters, she's got confidence in fucking spades.

I'm already sick of hearing of this stupid Cringey Craig guy, so I step in. "I would be happy to clear things up with Craig on the whole 'getting back together' thing." I look around much like he just did, pretending to be looking for the toolbag. I don't even know what this jackhole looks like. I see Emmy smiling next to me as I look though, and I'll gladly play this role for her.

Mr. King clears his throat. "That won't be necessary. Emmy, I'd like to find a time to talk tonight about some family matters."

At this, Emmy tenses up. Huh. I wonder what these "family matters" are.

"We will see," she replies, tight-lipped. She then excuses herself to the bar for another drink, leaving me and Mr. King standing awkwardly together. I just smile at him. He smooths down his suit jacket, tells me to have a good night before walking away.

"Two down," I mutter.

"Sorry I left you. I thought it would be the only way to get him to go away." Emmy slides into the seat she vacated moments ago but with another drink for each of us.

"No worries, he doesn't intimidate me."

"Really?" She cocks her eyebrow.

"Really. Should he?" I mimic her look. She shakes her head.

"No, I guess if you don't already know who he is, then you wouldn't be intimidated. He's pretty powerful and wealthy as hell, people are always either kissing his ass or shaking in their boots."

"Well, I guess I just followed your lead." I get the feeling that we are being watched. I try not to make a point to look around, so instead I lean in and kiss her on the cheek.

"What's that for?" she asks with a smile, playing it off like it's normal.

"We are being watched."

She nods in understanding. We continue on like this for a bit longer. When I no longer feel like we've got a shadow, I excuse myself to the restroom.

"I'll be lighting fast." I give her a peck on the lips this time. Damn. The PDA is starting to happen more and more.

"If I'm not here, I'll be out there. Depends on if I need to hide from anyone."

I chuckle as I head toward the restrooms I saw near the elevators.

After a few minutes, I reemerge from the restroom and head to the bar for another drink. Open bar? Hell yeah, I'm taking advantage. Emmy isn't at our table and I don't see her, so I head out to the terrace.

There are a lot more people mingling around and fortunately I don't see Emmy trapped into conversations without me. Unfortunately, I can't find her. So help me, if she left me here, I'm going to be pissed. But then, across the open space, I see her in the very corner. At first, I think she really is hiding. My anger from the possibility of her leaving me shifts to anger at the possibility that someone upset her. I start toward her. But as I get closer, I notice she does something on her phone. Is she texting someone? She's moving around the space strangely, like maybe she keeps dropping cell service. Whatever she's doing, I don't think she is texting because she's using her pointer finger in a swipe up motion.

Standing just out of her view, I study her. She's fucking gorgeous, but she's acting strangely right now. I don't know if I should laugh or be concerned. Just then, someone comes up next to me and shoves his hands in his pockets. I notice he's a little taller than me.

"She's a nut. But I love her." His voice is full of affection. I look to him and immediately I know this is Levi. They've got the same dark hair and strikingly similar facial features.

"You must be Levi. Congratulations on your engagement." I turn my gaze back to Emmy. She's standing still now. Feverishly tapping her screen.

"Thank you, and you must be Jake."

I nod.

"You two have created quite a stir tonight."

I cock an eyebrow but remain focused on Emmy. "Really? I haven't gotten the feeling anyone really cares we're here except for your parents. Hell, Cringey Craig hasn't even bothered us."

Levi laughs, I assume at my use of the nickname. "Kitty has a knack for stirring shit quietly. Craig is preparing himself. He'll circle then pounce soon enough. You've been talking to Becca I see, since I've known only her to use that nickname for him." I grunt in response.

What the fuck is she doing? She's got to be playing a game or something.

"The more interesting topic here is the fact that you clearly know about Craig, yet I don't know anything about you. Emmy tells me about a lot of shit. And she hasn't mentioned you."

I turn to him to show him the respect he isn't showing me. But he's playing big brother right now, I get it. "I work in her building, so it's not really something we want getting out so soon. So, we've kept it on the down low."

He pinches his lips but nods.

"What the heck is she doing?" I finally ask.

"What do you mean?" He is looking at me again. So, I turn my body slightly toward him. Maybe I'm being rude, but his tone was confused.

"I mean, what is she doing over there in the corner? She's acting funny." I cross my arms. Clearly, I'm not the only one who just saw her fist-pump the air.

He looks at me with confusion. "She's playing Digibot Go. It's like her favorite game and current obsession. How do you not know this?"

Shit. Clearly, he isn't in on our little agreement, I've got to turn this around.

"Well, we're still learning a lot about each other, maybe she wasn't ready to tell me about Digibot Go yet." I'm grasping. I've got no reason, other than the fact that we really don't know each other at all.

"My sister is a huge nerd and has never hidden the fact." If it's possible, he just used his big bro superpowers and grew a few intimidating inches. "The only reason I can think of that might make her hide such an important thing about herself is if she felt unsafe or judged by someone." Now he's glaring at me.

"Look, I love nerdy and I'm happy to hear she's got a thing for Digibots, but she isn't hiding that part of herself from me because she's scared I'll judge her." He deflates a little. "Honest, I dig your sister and all her quirks." He's almost back to normal height when his name is called from across the terrace. He lets out a breath through his nose. Before he leaves, he delivers one last warning.

"Emmy is one of a kind. She's amazing and deserves anything that makes her happy. You better not make life hard on her. You got me, Jake?"

Raising my hands in agreement, I say, "I got you."

He nods and walks away.

I shake it off. Clearly, I did not make a good impression on the brother. Then I realize that I did not make a good impression on the stepmother or father. Great. Good thing this whole thing is fake or else I'd be in a world of hurt if my girlfriend's family hated me after one night.

mmy

"So, just a heads-up, I'm pretty sure Levi doesn't approve," Jake says as he approaches me, just as I'm sliding my phone into my clutch. While he was gone, I avoided Craig and snuck out onto the terrace through the other set of doors. While I was avoiding further mingling, I decided to check my phone. Okay, that's not true. I was checking out Digibot Go. Turns out there was a Digibot club on the far end of the terrace. There was a siege happening, I couldn't resist. Only thing, I was pretty much on top of the club, so every time I moved the little notification to "walk closer" kept popping up. I probably looked like someone tied to a shitty cell service carrier.

"Oh, you met him? I haven't gotten to talk to him yet. What happened?" I frown. I honestly thought he and Levi would get along.

"Well, I asked him what you were doing over here in the corner and on your phone. It kinda pissed him off."

My face flushes when I realize that, to Jake—and anyone else, for that matter —I probably looked like a crazy person.

"What were you doing?"

I bite my lip at his question. "I was playing Digibot Go."

He studies me while I wait for him to get all judgy on me. I don't know why I've hidden it from him. I'm a proud nerd, I don't hide my nerd flag. Normally. But Jake has been so damn judgmental of me from the start, I just didn't want to hear his snarky comments on it.

He smiles. I wait for it.

"If you're anything other than Team Intuition then we can't be friends."

It takes everything in me to keep my jaw attached to my face and not falling to the floor. He knows Digibots. If so, why didn't he know what I was doing? The confusion must show on my face.

"I don't play Digibot Go, but I grew up as a Digibot handler."

If this wasn't a fake relationship, I would say I might have fallen for him a little bit just now.

I clear my throat and find my voice. "Yes, I'm Team Intuition. Yellow is my favorite color." He smiles at me and I know I'm doing the same. It's like we just realized we are in on a great inside joke. The moment is broken when the music from the speakers seems to get louder. Looking around, I notice that several couples are now dancing.

"Look, I'm sure Levi was just caught off guard. He's your typical protective big brother, so some of it might have just been to size you up."

"Maybe, but I think he's either onto us or suspects me of being a total douchecan who's treating you poorly."

"I'll talk to him." I pat his chest with assurance. A zing of heat shoots through me and up my arm. I can see he feels it too because his eyes fill with heat and he stares at my mouth. Then it's his turn to clear his throat.

"Let me get you a drink. I saw some new appetizers out, I'll grab us a plate."

I nod and watch him walk away. Lost in staring at Jake's fine backside, I'm caught off guard by Craig. And to my disdain, Kitty. *Great.*

"Baby doll, it's so good to see you. I've been looking for you all night." Craig opens his arms to me, expecting a hug. When I don't fall into him, he drops his arms, leans in, and kisses me on the cheek.

"Craig. I see you are doing well."

"Life is wonderful. I'm at the top of my career. I've finally moved on past the god-forsaken apartment living and bought a townhouse upstate. Near your parents actually." He smiles lovingly at Kitty and I want to gag.

"Sounds like life is just perfect." I play along.

"It would be, but I just need to check one last thing off my list."

Oh god, his fucking list. Really, the list is why we broke up. He had wanted me to fill the role of "beautiful wife" so he could check that off his "Must Have by Thirty" list.

I don't appease him by asking what he wants me to. Instead, I turn to Kitty. "I have not seen Levi all night. Is he sneaking off somewhere?" Kitty rolls her eyes at my question, but I needed to change the subject.

"It is an engagement party, Emmy. What do you expect?" I knew that was coming. "Why don't the two of you dance? Catch up." She nudges me toward Craig.

"That's a wonderful idea, Kitty." He holds out his hand to me.

"Eh, no, thank you. I'm here with my boyfriend." I slide a glare at Kitty. Why is she forcing this?

"Surely your date wouldn't mind a friendly dance between you and a lifelong friend. Go on." She all but pushes me this time.

"Fine. One dance, as friends. Do you understand me, Craig?" I stare him down, I hope he feels my warning deep in his arrogant soul.

He chuckles and looks at me like he would a silly dog before patting it on the head and saying, "good girl."

He pulls me on to the dance floor, once there, he surprises me by keeping a respectful distance between us.

"It's really great to see you, Emmy. I have missed you." He sounds sincere and I cock my head and stare at him.

I decide to reiterate my point. "I have a boyfriend."

He smiles sadly. "Yes, I know. But just know, I'm ready and waiting for you when whatever this thing is between the two of you is over."

His sentiment is incredibly nauseating, and I want to tell him that whatever is going on between me and Jake isn't ending anytime soon … but it is. Because what Jake and I have is fake. Before I can reply, our dance is interrupted. Jake, looking as confident as can be, stands next to us.

He looks directly at Craig when he says, "May I cut in?"

Craig looks defeated but drops his arms and steps away.

"Sorry it took me so long. I was intercepted by who I think was the bride."

"Thank you for saving me."

"Was it that bad?" he asks as he pulls me in to him, closer than I had been with Craig. I'm so close to him that his subtle scent fills my nose.

I fight back a sigh of contentment. "Nah, I think he's finally listening to me and not Kitty."

He nods with an understanding smile. I move just the slightest bit closer to him. We don't talk after that. We dance slowly as the music playing through the speakers serenades us. We are nearly cheek to cheek. My left hand rests on his back, the other is clasped in his. Suddenly, we're caught up in the moment; it's just me and Jake. The song comes to an end and I start to pull back just as he turns slightly to close the gap between us. We are *so* close.

"I'm not sure everyone here believes we are really a couple." I'm looking up into his eyes as he continues, "So, it might be time to sell it."

My gaze drops to his mouth. His full lips are so enticing right now as they curve into a slow, lazy smile.

"Okay."

I hear the word, but I don't know if I actually said it out loud. A second later his lips are on mine and I melt into him. His tongue swipes at my lips and I let him deepen the kiss. My hand slides up to the nape of his neck and I want to sink my fingers into his hair, but I'm holding my clutch. I don't know if it's me or him who moans, but it sounds distant. The hand that was just holding mine is now cupping my jaw.

His kiss is sweet and slow. His mouth is soft on mine but also firm. It's an inviting combination. When his tongue swipes, just once across my own, it's warm and I worry my knees are about to buckle underneath me. I suddenly find myself wishing we were alone. I want nothing more than to take this kiss further. But reality sets in and I remember where we are. I break the kiss. Dazed, I peek up at Jake, he only looks smug.

Stunned from the kiss, I panic. "I need to use the ladies' room." I'm surprised I don't stumble as I turn in the search for my escape. I could use some space to clear my head because I'm wondering how much of that kiss was fake and how much of it was real. Whatever tension there is between us is starting to get out of hand, and we need to get it in check.

There isn't a line for the single-stall ladies' room, and once I'm inside I take a deep breath. Staring at myself in the mirror, I let out a few more.

"What are you doing, Em?" I say to myself. "What did you expect? He's being paid a shit ton of money. He's committed to his job." Just then a knock comes at the door. "Just a minute," I say loudly over the water I just turned on.

"Emmy, it's me. Let me in." Jake's gravelly voice filters through the door, and without thinking, I open it. With a glance over his shoulder, he slips into the luxurious bathroom.

Instead of asking him why he's here, I go with another question instead. "What was that out there?"

"I told you, we needed to sell this whole being a couple act." He looks perplexed by my question. I'm still breathing heavy and I'm not quite sure if I'm still worked up from the kiss or if I'm just annoyed about the situation.

"Yeah, but that was more than just a kiss. It didn't need to go that far."

"Look, I didn't like the way Craig was looking at you while we were dancing. When he wasn't sizing me up like I was his competition, he couldn't keep his eyes off your ass." Jake's not one bit phased with the fact that he just admitted to being jealous of Craig.

Crossing my arms, I shake my head and say, "Even so, a simple kiss would have sufficed."

"So, what? You saying you didn't enjoy it?" He smirks, knowing damn well I enjoyed it. But I give in because there is no use trying to be mad when my heart is racing, and my lips are still tingling. Fretting about this is a waste of breath ... I'm not even sure why I'm making a big deal about it.

I sigh and drop my arms, my small bag slapping against my thigh. "No. It was the most amazing kiss, too bad there was nothing real about it."

His eyes heat and his smirk drops away.

"What are you doing in here, anyway?" I ask. But instead of an answer, I get his mouth slamming into mine.

My clutch tumbles to the floor as I wrap my arms around his neck. His tongue delves into my mouth as he lifts me onto the counter. Instinctively, I wrap my legs around his waist.

This kiss is passionate and reckless. My fingers dig into his hair as he pulls me to the edge of the counter. With one arm wrapped around my waist, he slides his other hand across my hip and down my thigh, hiking my leg up higher on his hip. The feeling of his hot, rough hands on my bare thigh pulls a moan from me. And that moan is all the permission he needs to keep going.

His hand slides further up my thigh, delving under my dress. I feel it slowly crawl across my hot skin. I'm on fire everywhere he touches. When his fingers reach the apex of my thigh, I gasp in anticipation. The need for him to go further is undeniable. He pauses only for the slightest moment before he brushes his finger over my lace-covered sex. Once, then twice before his thumb dips under the lace. A moan escapes him as he feels how molten hot I am for him.

Sliding my palms to either side of his neck, I can't seem to get close enough. I slide my tongue against his, tasting a hint of whiskey. Growling, he palms my breast through my dress. I tug at the hem of his shirt, wanting nothing between us. Suddenly, there's a knock on the door. I jump and Jake takes a giant step back. I look to the door as I hear my brother from the other side.

"Might want to consider just getting a room." Levi doesn't say anything else, so I assume he walked away.

Still trying to catch my breath, I lean over and turn off the faucet. Jake stands there, almost looking angry, his chest straining against his shirt with each heaving breath. Color me confused because it sure felt like he was enjoying what was just happening.

I repeat my earlier question, "What was that?"

He shakes his head. "I don't know." He breaks eye contact and adjusts himself through his pants. "But I think it's time for me to take you home."

He brushes past me and lets himself out of our bubble of lust.

I can tell by his behavior now that he doesn't mean we'll be continuing this later at my apartment. Whatever he may think that was just now, it most certainly did not feel fake.

ake

I GLANCE at my phone as it rings and decide to let another call from Emmy go to voicemail. It's been a little more than a week since the engagement party. I haven't seen or heard from Emmy until yesterday. It had been radio silence for the both of us after I dropped her off at her apartment. I wasn't very gentlemanly about it either. I was so caught up in my head about what the hell had happened with us in the ladies' room that I pushed the door open, helped her out of the cab, told her good night and that was it. I watched from the cab as she made it inside the building and then had the taxi take me home.

At first, I only received a couple of texts from her, about needing to talk to me about the shower coming up this weekend. Then last night, she called me. She left a huffy message about needing a quick chat. I hate to admit it, but I've been hiding from her. I've been on call, but I'm not the only one. I've asked some of the other guys to take any calls that have been near her floor or in public areas throughout the building. But I need to get over it and find her since the shower is in a few days.

I guess I've been avoiding her because I don't want to talk about our make out. It was fucking hot, and I was so into it. Until I remembered that she is a Madison resident, not to mention she was paying me to be her fake boyfriend. Clearly, I'm attracted to her, but I needed to put some space between us. I don't blame her for being huffy at me.

Cut to today. There's an issue with one of the elevators, some buttons need to be replaced. Since I'm the only one here right now, I can't delegate the task to someone else. I'm going to have to stop hiding.

I don't even get both feet out of the maintenance office when I come face-to-face with a hopping-mad Emmy.

"Oh, so you weren't abducted by aliens?" Emmy stands there in a cream-colored dress. The heels she's wearing show off her killer legs—legs I had wrapped around me just a week ago. She must be coming from work since I know what she wears around her apartment and this isn't it. I can't decide which look I prefer. Her professional look or her laid-back, couldn't-care-less look. I do know that her "out on the town" look from the other night nearly knocked me on my ass.

"Nope. Just stupid busy with work." I pull my gaze away from her sexy figure and walk right on past her. "I'm actually on my way to fix the elevator."

She follows me. I knew she would, she clearly has a bone to pick. This should be fun.

"Right. Well, you're ghosting me, and I don't like it."

I fight back an answering grin. She's cute when she's mad.

"Whatever. Look, I need to talk to you about the shower. The venue changed last minute, it's now at my parents' house. I just wanted to prepare you but since you're too busy being an ass, that's fine too."

I can't help it, her sass is fun. I just keep ignoring her as I stop at the elevator in need of repair. I open it up and turn the key to shut it down. The door will be stuck in the open position until I'm done with my work. While I'm in the giant metal box, she teeters right outside. She crosses her arms and pops out her hip when I don't say anything.

"I don't know what your problem is, and I don't care, but you don't get to be a jerk to me."

I steal a glance at her, and while she looks pissed, I can see a tiny bit of vulnerability in her eyes. She's hurt by the way I've behaved since attacking her mouth. Her fucking delicious mouth.

I sigh and give her my full attention. "You're right, I'm sorry. It won't happen again." As soon as I say this, I realize I didn't specify which reason I'm apologizing for, the "being a jerk and ghosting her" part, or the "making out with her" part. If I'm honest, I don't know which one either.

She registers the wording and her expression goes blank. "Good. You have a job to do, so buck up and do it."

Of course, a reminder about what this thing between us really is. A business transaction. I roll my eyes as I turn back to the button panel in the elevator. "Look, this will take me just a few minutes to fix. If you wait for me over in the lobby, we can talk when I'm done." I nod to the plush couches across the way.

She doesn't say a word but turns and walks toward them. I pretend to not watch those legs I've been dreaming about for the past seven nights as they glide away from me.

I keep up my end of the deal and head over to the couch once I've completed the elevator repair. She's sitting on a couch, with her legs crossed at the ankles, staring at her phone. I recognize the upwards swipe of her finger on the phone and can't help the smile.

She's playing Digibots for sure.

"Catching anything good?" I come to a stop in front of her.

Looking up at me, she gives me a slight smile and shakes her head. "Nothing I don't already have."

She clicks off her phone and stands, bringing us face-to-face. I can smell her light perfume and it's enough to make my mouth water, along with the thoughts of me kissing along her neck and breathing in that sweet scent.

"I'm going to have to download the game. My brother, Kevin, plays and was just telling me about some kind of new feature." I'm telling her the truth, but I'm also extending an olive branch.

"Yeah, you can now fight other handlers, it's really pretty cool." Her earlier anger seems to have melted away, I'll have to file this in my Emmy bank, talking about Digibots makes her happy.

"So, tell me about the shower. What's going on?"

She starts to say something right as I hear an all-too-familiar voice, one I don't want to deal with. Crazy Sara from the fourteenth floor.

"Oh, Jake!" her voice rings out from somewhere behind us.

I suck in a breath, look into Emmy's waiting eyes and mouth, "I'm sorry." Then I turn to face a very enthusiastic Sara.

I've been lucky, so freaking lucky that I haven't run into her since our date. I've been avoiding her floor. Granted, I haven't seen her at all and there haven't been any work orders come in for her unit, so like I said, I've been lucky.

"Sara, hey, how are you?" She looks do damn happy to see me, I'm at a complete loss for words. I thought it was pretty clear when I faked an emergency that I wasn't interested.

"I'm doing great." Right as she says this, Emmy shifts out from behind me.

I turn my head to look at her and see a look of pure curiosity on her face. Sara comes to an abrupt stop and throws a stink eye Emmy's way. Oh no, it's like the crazy switch was just flipped.

She looks right at Emmy when she speaks. "Jakey, I hope Grammy is doing well, I hope her fall wasn't too bad. I was so worried after her last spell." She drags her dagger-crazed eyes toward me now.

"Oh, yeah, Grammy is just fine."

Emmy steps up next to me now, her interest piqued.

Reaching out, Sara touches my arm. "That's wonderful news."

I just nod in agreement. I can see it on her face that whatever is about to come out of her mouth is going to be a doozy.

"So, baby, when can we meet up again?" She starts to caress my arm now. She's also fluttering her lashes.

"Uh, do you have something in your eye?" I attempt and fail.

"Our last date was just so hot, that little handyman of yours has been on my mind. I can't wait for another go at him." Her voice is sultry and deep, she winks.

My mind is blown by the lies that are just falling out of her mouth.

"And those hands," she moans as her eyes flutter shut, "those rough hands on my soft skin, it was perfection."

She's completely crazy and I'm not about to let Emmy think this shit really happened.

Next to me, Emmy straightens.

I shift a little so I'm out of Sara's reach, and she finally drops her arm.

"Sara, that's not what—" I begin, just before Emmy steps in.

She pulls me to her and links her arm through mine. "Sara was it?"

Sara leans back, clearly offended. "Yes."

"Well, unfortunately, another date with Jake and his little handyman and rough hands isn't in the cards for you."

"And why not?" Sara's fist flies to her hip and she nearly stomps.

"Because Jake and I are a thing now."

Sara narrows her eyes at us, then focuses those crazy things on me, "How serious of a thing?"

Emmy answers for me, "Dead serious. He met my parents last week."

Sara's eyes go wide at Emmy's admission. I was worried Sara wasn't going to believe her, and I was going to have to kiss Emmy again. I know, it's a hardship, but I'm willing to take one for the team.

Huffing, Sara shakes her head and looks disappointed. "Well, I guess now just wasn't our time, Jake."

It's my turn to look at her in shock. She keeps going.

"I wish you the best of luck in life. If your little handyman ever misses me, let me know. I can be discreet." With that, she turns and walks toward the elevators.

My jaw ... it hits the floor.

I can almost see the steam pouring out of Emmy's ears. She starts to go after Sara, but I yank her back by her arm and place a hand on her waist. "Hey, hey, calm down. You're better than that," I say quietly into her ear.

"That woman just offered to be the other woman. To help you cheat." She's glaring down Sara's retreating form.

"I know, but I'm not a cheater and never will be. I'm also not interested in her."

She shakes me off, my arms drop to my sides. God, she's adorable when she's mad. Having to hold her back from a possible cat fight has my body excited. Cat fights are not my thing, but when it's Emmy trying to defend my honor, it's a whole different ball game.

Emmy shakes her head as if to bring herself back to the moment. "Why do I even care?" She gestures between us. "We aren't real."

"Then why'd you get so jealous?" I prod.

What? It's what men do, we like to push buttons, it can't be helped.

"No! I wasn't jealous! I was trying to help you out." She's all flustered now. Adorable.

"Right, if you say so, Emmy." I can't help my smug smile.

She lets out a frustrated growl. "Well, now your no-screwing-the-residents rule makes sense. You shacked up with the building's crazy and now you're playing it safe."

"Hey now, be nice. I didn't fuck Sara." She shoots me a look of disbelief. "Not for a lack of trying on her end though. Hell, Emmy, she named my dick!"

Emmy presses her lips together.

"I found her on some hookup app and didn't realize who she was until about two minutes after our date started. She drove right on in to crazy town after that."

"Then how does she know your grammy?" My grammy will get a kick out of this story later, that's for sure.

"She doesn't, she was trying to make you jealous."

Emmy's eye twitches at the comment.

"Less than thirty minutes into our date, I called my brother and faked an emergency. That's the story I gave her."

She studies me. I think she believes me.

"The date was that bad?" She bites her lip.

"The worst. She wasted no time letting me know how hot she was for me. She's one very horny and crazy woman."

She thinks about it then lets out a resigned huff. "I believe you, not that it matters." She grumbles the last part.

"It does matter," I tell her gently. As hot as she is when she's acting all jealous and shit, there's no reason for her to be jealous of Sara.

"No, it doesn't, Jake. We're fake." She looks me right in the eyes when she says it. Her matter-of-fact tone sounds almost sad, and it hits me straight in the middle of my chest.

"Emmy—" I start.

"What are you doing on a hookup app anyway? Are you a man whore?" Now she's pushing *my* buttons. I roll my eyes. "I should be glad for your no-screwing-the-residents rule. I don't want any STDs that's for sure."

"Whoa, whoa, hold up. I'm not a man whore and I don't have any STDs." This conversation is getting way off track. I continue to defend my virtue, "I just don't have time to date, so when I need to ... you know ... I use the app. Wham, bam, thank you, ma'am."

"*Ick* ... Whatever. I'm done here." She waves me off with disgust and heads for the elevators herself. I'm left standing there in the lobby watching her leave.

"Well, that was one enjoyable shitshow," Thomas, the daytime doorman, says from where he's leaning up against the security desk. He must have just taken a break because he's normally stationed at the doors.

I chuckle and shake my head. "Yeah, it was."

I head back toward the maintenance office and think about her last comment. *"I should be glad for your no-screwing-the-residents rule."* Does that mean what I think it means?

Shit. If screwing Emmy King wasn't already the number one thing on my mind, it sure is now.

mmy

A FEW DAYS after the Sara incident in the lobby, Jake and I are in an Uber on our way to my childhood home. A place I haven't been in five years. My nerves are nearly shot and mix in the fact that I can smell Jake's cologne isn't helping. I'm still annoyed with him ignoring my texts and call the week following our hot and heavy make-out session at The Rooftop. It was clearly something more than he is willing to admit since he ran and hid from me. Massive man-baby.

I'd be lying if I didn't at least admit to myself that I'd like a repeat, but not until after we've discussed what was really going on between us. I'm a forever kind of girl but he's just into one-night hookups. I'm not. I've had casual sex plenty of times before. But I've never had the connection with them that I do with Jake. I want to be around him. I want to learn more about him. I've been happy when I'm with him, aside from that one time when there was a crazy-eyed psycho trying to make me jealous. Which she didn't, by the way.

Fine. Maybe a little. Or a lot.

Either way, I like being with him and I'm thankful he's here to have my back as we enter the lion's den.

Kitty out in public is tame. Kitty in her headquarters is another beast entirely.

"Emmy, if you don't stop twisting the strap, you're going to break it." I look down at what Jake is referring to, and sure enough, the strap of my clutch purse is wound so tight it's about to snap. Which ironically, is exactly how I feel right now. As I stare down at the strap, his hand covers both of mine and he weaves his fingers through one of them, gripping it tightly.

I take a deep breath. I look to him, but he's looking out the window at the passing streets. I feel the last of my annoyance with him from the past week slip away as I realize that he isn't here to calm me, but he does anyway.

"So, your family home is that bad, eh?" He turns and smiles at me this time.

I take another deep breath. "Yes, if you thought Kitty was bad at the engagement party, then she'll be worse here."

He nods in understanding. "And Craig … will he be there?" His grip on my hand tightens a fraction.

"No, I don't think so, Craig told me he would back off." I fight off a chill thinking back on that conversation.

Jake just grunts in reply. "Even if he is, we've got this, right?"

I smile and lift our hands, giving them a shake.

He chuckles this time. "That's right, baby." And brings our clasped hands over to cross his lap. I can't stop the tingles that shoot up my arm and then continue through my entire body.

Moments later we arrive at the King home.

Jake lets out a whistle and I groan, "Welcome to the King mansion. A.K.A. Hell."

He steps out of the car first, adjusting his sleeves and buttoning his jacket. It's the same navy-blue one from last week but today he's wearing a striped, light-blue button-up underneath it. It all matches surprisingly well with a pair of light-salmon-colored dress pants. I told him he didn't have to get the pink pants, but he really liked them. His whole outfit matches mine perfectly. I pieced mine together for under fifty dollars, thanks to a few discount stores. The light-pink tulle skirt with a matching shimmery pink top and my favorite new denim jacket. It's definitely a more fun and carefree outfit.

Kitty will probably hate it which almost makes me giddy.

He holds his hand out to me as I scoot across the back seat of the car. I take his hand as he helps me out. I brush the back of my skirt down and look up at him.

He's watching me intently.

"You look beautiful, Emmy." My hand is still in his and he brings it up to his lips and kisses the back of my hand.

Cue more tingles.

"Are you ready?" he asks as he lowers our hands but doesn't let go.

"It's now or never." We start walking up the steps and I mumble, "It's been five years, how bad can it be?" My words don't go unnoticed, he lifts an eyebrow, but I ignore it and knock on the massive, dark wood, front door.

It opens immediately and a maid I don't recognize ushers us in.

The obnoxious clacking of her heels announces her entrance before her words and I remind myself to keep my cool. "Emerson, nice of you to join us. I see you remembered how to get here."

"That was fast," Jake whispers. Kitty appears out of thin air before the door behind us is even closed.

I bite back a smile. Yes, yes, it was. "I lived here for eighteen years, Kitty, I don't suspect I'll ever forget," I mutter, leaning in to kiss her cheek while she does the same.

When she's done with the pleasantries, she grips my forearms and studies my outfit. She makes a snooty sound from her nose. "What are you wearing, Emerson? You look like a beach bum." I call it a win when she drops her hands and gives her attention to Jake, who straightens his shoulders. "Jake, it's lovely to see you again."

I'm impressed she's saying nice things even though she clearly doesn't mean them because the disdain on her face is hard to miss.

"Mrs. King, you have a lovely home."

She nods in agreement just as another knock comes at the door behind us. "Oh, please, Emmy, don't crowd the door." She shoos us away.

"I'm ready for that drink now." Jake chuckles in my ear.

I drag him through the grand entryway into the parlor where one of my father's many small bars is located. It's stocked with all the standard alcohol but for today's event it even boasts a bartender.

Over the next hour or so, Jake's hand never leaves the small of my back. He stands close and whispers in my ear a commentary of what he sees. The room is filled with people gossiping and kissing ass. It's comical yet sad to see it from an outsider's perspective. This is a life I don't miss at all.

He jokes and kisses my cheek. When we sit to watch Darcy and Levi open gifts, he holds my hand. The warmth between us is obvious, I just don't know if it's real. Is this all for show? Or is it because he can't keep his hands to himself? I'm not sure I'm going to be able to get through another two events with him without knowing where we stand outside of this fake boyfriend gig. I'd be an idiot to think this is anything other than what it was supposed to be.

After the gifts are opened, Jake looks for the bathroom while people scatter for cake. After directing him to the spacious half bath, I turn around and find Levi is walking toward me. We chat for several minutes. Even though it's about nothing special, it's nice to feel like myself for a few moments and not like I am in a cage or on display. Just as I realize that Jake's been gone longer than I would have expected, Darcy's mother pulls Levi away. After standing there for another minute longer, I take one last look at my watch and decide to go find my fake boyfriend. I'm assuming he probably got lost in the crowded maze of this house. The hall toward the bathroom is tucked back and away from the parlor, so there are not many people walking around. Just as I'm about to turn the corner, I stop when I hear Jake's voice.

"Look, I'm really not interested." He sounds firm.

"Oh, come on. A man like you, you must be interested." It's Darcy's voice I hear in response.

My eyes narrow.

"Darcy, you're a very pretty woman, but I'm dating Emmy. I like her a lot and the last thing I'm going to do is jeopardize that relationship." I peek around the corner. They are facing each other, neither one sees me. Jake removes Darcy's hand from his chest. "Not to mention, you're getting married to Emmy's brother."

"It's alright, no one has to know. I've been watching you, Jake, and I'm interested." Honestly, it doesn't surprise me that Darcy is making a play at Jake. She did this kind of thing all through high school. She was always stealing other girls' boyfriends. Or at least tried to. I was quite surprised when I found out Levi was marrying her. She's bad news.

I contemplate helping him out, but he doesn't need it. "You need to walk away, or I'll have to tell Levi."

She huffs and snaps back, "Fine, you couldn't handle this"—she waves her hand down the length of her body—"anyways." She turns to stomp away, and I realize she's coming right toward me. I panic and scurry back the way I came, ducking behind a large floor vase at the last minute. Peeking through the wisps of plant leaves, I see her turn into the hallway that leads to the kitchen. I sigh with relief as I straighten and head back for Jake.

As I turn the corner, I see him standing in the same spot as before but he's facing away from me. His hands are in his hair and he's clearly agitated. When I get a little closer I hear his voice. He's mumbling to himself, "Fuuuck. I've got to tell her."

I smile. He's so cute, all worried and stressed out. I could play the whole, clueless act, but games aren't my thing. Clearly, he's upset and knows he's got to tell me.

"Wow, you are a man whore." I chuckle. I might not like mind games, but I'm one hundred percent on board with teasing.

Jake whips around to face me, looking stunned at first until he catches my smile. His shoulders sag in relief. "You heard all of that, didn't you?" He leans back against the wall, I come up next to him and do the same. We are shoulder to shoulder. I don't know when it happened, but it's like our bodies are magnetic.

"I did. Not all of it, just the part where you told her to pretty much back off."

He sighs. "You don't sound surprised." He turns his head toward me, one eyebrow raised.

"Unfortunately, I'm not. I went to school with Darcy. She has a reputation. That's why I couldn't believe Levi was marrying her. Once a cheater, always a cheater." I lean into him. "Good news is, it's clear you are not. You've had what? Two women in just the past few days offering to ... help you out? You going for a record or something?"

"Or something." He grins.

Pushing off the wall, I grab his hand. "Come on, we have to tell Levi."

"I was hoping you weren't going to say that. Levi and I didn't quite get off on the right foot when we first met. This won't help matters," Jake grumbles, but I pull him down the hall anyway.

Looking back over my shoulder I tell him, "It will be fine. Promise." Then I wink.

"I have the sudden urge to pull you into the bathroom right now," he grumbles in reply. I nearly halt and take him up on his offer just as a teenage girl that I recognize as one of my stepsister, Ashley's, friends walks past us and disappears into said bathroom. Maybe later then.

As I weave through the small groups of people back in the parlor, Darcy is nowhere to be found. Levi is easy to spot though.

"Levi, can we talk?" I tap on his shoulder.

He turns and I can tell he's thankful for the interruption. His gaze flickers to Jake, his facial expression hardens just a smidge, but nods. Maybe I should be worried about his dislike for Jake. I lead us all out past the parlor through the house to the back. I always forget how big this place is in comparison to my shared apartment. I take us to a small study that Kitty likes to call hers. She has to have a place to plan all those fundraisers she handles for the Junior League.

Jake walks over to the leather couch and sits down. Well, he might as well be comfortable for this awkward conversation we are about to have.

"What's up, sis?" Levi says, closing the door behind him.

"I just want to preface this by saying that I love you and your happiness means the world to me," I tell him.

Levi chuckles and walks over near the big oak desk and leans against it.

I remain standing, because I'm about to deliver bad news.

"Right, got it." He crosses his arms but still appears relaxed.

"So, just now ... well, about fifteen minutes ago, Darcy tried to proposition Jake for a little tryst in the bathroom. He said no, obviously, but we felt you needed to know."

He studies me then Jake. I fight off my urge to fidget.

"And he told you this happened?" He nods toward Jake, like maybe he doesn't believe us.

"I saw it happen." I cross my own arms because I'm not sure I like his tone. I love my brother, but I'm going to defend Jake if need be.

Levi doesn't say anything right way, he just studies me. Then he looks down at his black, perfectly polished shoes.

"Are you going to say anything?" I can't help my annoyed tone.

He lifts a shoulder, quite casually in my opinion. "I'm not surprised, it's really not a big deal. Nothing happened, so we can move on."

Uh, what?

I take a step back, feeling like I was just hit with a two-by-four. "I'm sorry, but why are you not mad?"

"Because I'm not?" His tone matches my questioning one.

"Why?" I'm mad for him, why isn't he freaking mad?!

He sighs. "Look, Ems, thank you for telling me, but it's really not a big deal." There is an expression that I can't read on his face. Is he defeated? Does he look relieved? I don't know. I just don't understand why…

Oh…

"She's done this before to you, hasn't she?"

He shrugs, emotionless.

"And you're just okay with your soon-to-be wife not even waiting for the ink to dry on the marriage certificate before she starts cheating?"

"It is what it is, Ems."

"Bullshit, Levi," I whisper-yell. "You're going to marry Darcy and you're completely okay with her cheating on you? You just don't do that to the one you love!"

"Keep your voice down, Emmy," he hisses, and I roll my eyes. No one will hear us back here.

"And who said anything about love?" he mutters.

"Oh, so let me guess, this is Dad's doing? Right? You're not marrying for love, you're marrying for money?" I can't help but snarl at the thought.

"Don't give me that—*don't* judge me," he bites back.

"See, this is why I got out."

"Give me a break, it's not like we're in the mob. Stop being dramatic. Unlike you, I'm not interested in walking away from millions just to be happy. You know what? Money *can* buy fucking happiness. But then, you wouldn't know, since you don't have any anymore," he snaps.

That's when I hear a shift beside me on the couch. That's when I remember that Jake has been watching this whole shitshow of an argument.

And now he knows my truth.

CHAPTER 14

Jake

DID I HEAR THAT CORRECTLY? I shift in my seat, suddenly feeling overheated.

I don't think I understand what I am hearing right now. Emmy got out? She walked away from money? But she has money, lots of it. She lives in the 425 Madison building, for Christ's sake. Plus, she dropped a grand on clothes for me and her own clothes are all designer.

This doesn't make sense. She has money—not that I care, I don't have a lot of money, and I'm not a fucking gold digger.

No, what doesn't make sense is that she would lie to me about it. Why would she let me believe that she has money when she doesn't? Why would she offer to pay me fifteen grand to be her fake boyfriend?

What the actual fuck? There has got to be some kind of explanation here. One that doesn't result in my anger quietly boiling up within me.

I shoot a look to Emmy and she's standing stock-still, her eyes closed. I swing my gaze to Levi and see that he's studying her as well.

"Wait a second. Wait one-fucking-second." Levi pushes off the desk, walks over to the couch I'm sitting on, and plops down at the other end. Once he's comfortable he continues. "What's going on here?"

I stare hard at Emmy, willing her to look at me. She doesn't.

"So, let me get this straight, you're getting all up in my business about starting a marriage built on infidelity, yet you're starting a relationship out on a bed of lies? Interesting."

He's a dick. I don't know why Emmy thinks the world of this guy. Brother or not.

"We aren't starting our relationship out with lies." Emmy grits her teeth.

Levi looks between us for a few seconds. "Clearly something shady is happening right now. You look guilty as shit and Jake, well, he looks fucking clueless."

"Fuck off, Levi," Emmy spits.

This guy is really pissing me off.

The tool just smiles. He's clearly enjoying this.

"Something isn't right here. What is it? I've been curious about the two of you from the start. What … is … it." He steeples his fingers and brings them to his mouth. His eyes ping-pong between us as he tries to work things out.

It takes mere seconds, but it feels like years. Centuries.

"*Shit.*" He leans back in his seat, his mouth wide, palms pressed to his temples. He's figured it out. "This thing between the two of you, it's not real, is it?"

Emmy's shoulders sag at Levi's revelation but he doesn't notice.

"I knew it. I knew something wasn't right."

Emmy squeaks, "How?"

"Simple, Jake didn't know jack-squat about you and … damn. I knew it." He lets out a little chuckle to himself.

My anger simmers for a second and then annoyance replaces it. We did a fan-fucking-tastic job selling the whole boyfriend-girlfriend thing.

"Oh god, so what if I didn't know she plays Digibot Go?" I grumble and roll my eyes.

Levi just ignores me.

"Well, look at that, little sister. Seems like you still care very much about what this life you keep running from thinks of you."

84

Emmy stands in the middle of the room. She's trying to regain some of her composure, but I can tell by the tension in her shoulders that she's fighting to stand tall.

When she doesn't answer, he continues, "Tell me, Ems, what's in it for him? Surely not money, since you've got none. What is it then? Sex? You paying him with sex?" His words are like venom and she flinches.

I've had enough.

I stand from the couch, point a menacing finger and glare in his direction. "Don't you dare speak to her like that again."

He has enough common sense to recognize that he has taken it too far. He curses under his breath. "Emmy, shit. I'm sorry." He at least looks remorseful.

Emmy nods to Levi. She has unshed tears in her eyes when she finally makes eye contact with me. I stop in front of her, too mad to really comfort her.

"Looks like you have some explaining to do. I'm not doing it here with an audience. So, let's go." I raise an eyebrow in challenge, but she just nods in agreement. I don't bother grabbing her hand as I head for the door. I also don't bother with any pleasantries on my way out of the house.

I pull out my phone to order an Uber. Looks like we've got a seven-minute wait.

By the time I slide my phone back into my pocket, Emmy joins me on the steps. I stand at the bottom of them, she sits a few rows up.

"Jake, I'm so sorry for what happened in there." She brings her arms up around her middle, hugging herself.

"What the fuck, Emmy? What haven't you been telling me?" I growl but just then the front door opens.

An older couple descend the stairs, I assume to leave. I realize the last thing I want to do is have this conversation in front of gossiping assholes.

"I guess I haven't been completely honest with you," she mutters but watches the couple walk to their car.

"I don't want to talk about this here."

She nods in agreement and I stay where I'm at. I need some space. I'm drawn to her like a moth to a flame, I want to comfort her and tell her it doesn't matter that Levi knows about our arrangement. But I can't because she's been lying to me. Too bad I don't date liars.

Nearly an hour later, after one of the longest car rides ever, the car pulls up in front of 425 Madison.

"Are you coming up?" Her hand is on the door handle and I can't tell in the dark, shadowed car if she wants me to or not. What I do know is that I need to know what the hell she's hiding from me and I need to know tonight.

All I can give her is a yes, and then I follow her out of the car. Several long, tense minutes later, Emmy and I enter her dark and empty apartment.

"Where's Becca?" I can't help but look over at the Skee-Ball machine. I think about how I'd much rather play a few rounds of that than have the conversation we are about to have.

"She's visiting her cousin for the weekend." She tosses her purse on the table and leans down to take off her heels.

I force myself to look away. I so badly wish we were up here to do something more enjoyable. Skee-Ball sure, but I've had to stare at those sexy legs and that hot-as-hell mouth all night. And I want to touch, and I want to taste. I want it all. But I can't want it all if there's something she's keeping from me. All those things I want, all the sexual fantasies that have been stacking up will never happen if I don't know the real Emmy King.

She walks over to the couch and plops down. She's barefoot and still dressed in her shimmery pink outfit. "Sit, please?" Her eyes are remorseful, and I'm drawn to her, even through my anger and confusion. So, I sit on the couch. As far away from her as I can.

"I'm really sorry about what happened tonight, about how the conversation with Levi turned out." She hesitates but doesn't continue.

"I want to know what you walked away from. I want to know about why you really don't get along with your family." I cross my arms and lean back, waiting for answers.

She gulps and then takes a deep breath, readying herself to give her explanation. "When I graduated college, I walked away from my family's money, my trust fund."

I process that and then ask, "What do you mean you walked away?"

"I mean, I never accessed my trust when I turned twenty-five. I opted out of joining the family business so I could live by my own terms. Because of that, I no longer have access to my parents' money."

I shake my head. "I don't understand what the big deal is."

She sighs. "When I declared my independence, I went against everything my father had planned for me. When you grow up with a silver spoon in your mouth, you're not supposed to spit it out." She shrugs a shoulder. "I did. And no one from that world understood. I was the talk of the town. A disgraced high-society princess, if you will. Kitty couldn't spin enough shit to sweep our dirty laundry under the rug. No, I was a hot topic, the gossip mill was turning. My father was furious. He said I was betraying him. And Levi never understood how I could walk away from the only life I knew. But supported my decision because he's my brother."

"Well, you do work for a competitor." I point this out, but it's unimportant. I'm just buying myself time to process what she's saying.

"Kind of." She acts like she's had this argument before, but I don't care to open that can of worms.

"What about Becca?"

"Loved me no matter what. She'd never walk away from her trust, but that doesn't mean she hasn't had my back from the start."

I think over everything she just shared for a few seconds. There's still one fact that I'm hung up on.

"You lied to me," I spit out. My thoughts keep circling back to that fact. She freaking lied to me. "Why did you let me believe you were made of money? I thought I knew you. I thought all the stuff you've told me about yourself was the truth. I don't even know what's real anymore." She fucking lied to me. After all the bullshit my mom went through with my dickhead of a father, leaving us after finding out about his "second" family, I can't find it in me to easily forgive a liar. No matter how unimportant.

"It was only as real as you were going to allow it to be."

"So, it's my fault you've been lying to me? Nice." I shake my head. I don't believe this shit right now. I push off the couch.

"That's not what I said. From the start you made it known how you felt about my *type*." She air quotes the last word. "With offhanded comments, requesting more money and expensive clothes, and your stupid no-screwing-the-residents rule, you made it clear you didn't ever want this to be real."

I start for the door, but I'm not done. I turn back toward her. "For someone who doesn't care about what other people think about her why the hell would you let me believe such a lie?"

She lifts a shoulder. "I thought we were pretending. You were pretending to be my fake boyfriend and I the rich trust-fund brat you assumed me to be."

"That's bullshit," I bellow and stop the tracks I was making back and forth across her floor.

She stands and squares her shoulders but doesn't make a move to come closer to me. "No, it's not. You're the one that started changing the tone of this"—she waves a hand between us—"thing between us. Kissing me and touching me. I can feel the desire pouring off of you when I stand too close. You made this more than what it was ever supposed to be."

Shit.

"You're right. I want you so fucking bad. I'm so fucking attracted to you that I can barely handle being in the same room with you, let alone standing right next to you. I'm drawn to you and I thought I was getting to know you more and more each time we were together. And now I've come to find that you've fucking lied to me about everything." I can't help yelling. I'm so frustrated. My mind is telling me to be livid, my body ... well, something else entirely.

"I lied about one thing, Jake. That I don't have money. Everything I own, I bought it with my own hard-earned money. Why are you so angry to find that out?" The volume of her voice nearly matches mine from just moments ago. She crosses her arms and juts out a hip like *she* is the one who gets to be mad at *me*.

"You live here in the god damn 425 Madison building. You wear designer clothes." My brain is still trying to connect the dots. I feel like a toddler unable to understand such a simple concept.

"Becca owns this apartment. I pay her deeply discounted rent each month. And these clothes"—she flicks the denim jacket she's wearing—"I get them from discount stores and secondhand shops. Why does it matter so much that I don't have money? Are you worried you're not going to get paid? I made a deal with you, you'll get your money."

I just shake my head because I don't care about that.

"Are you mad because you were only into me because you thought I had money?" She doesn't yell this, but her tone is coarser.

"Fuck no! If anything, I want you more," I hiss back at her. *Shit.* I can't believe I just said that. But it's out there now.

"What?" Her voice is now a near whisper.

"I refuse to be with someone who has the ability to make me feel bad about my upbringing. My childhood was hard, but I wouldn't change it. I've dated one-too-many women who were never going to be happy with some poor maintenance man. Every high-society brat I ever dated couldn't handle how everyone looked down on me because I worked with my hands and not with my mind in some stuffy business suit. But you … you come from money yet you walked away from all of it so you could be a normal person, which makes you more like me than anyone else I've ever dated."

She ponders this for a moment. Her chest rises and falls with each heavy breath. I want to kiss her so badly right now.

"Then why are you so mad at me?" Confusion is thick around her words. I suddenly realize that we are standing nearly chest to chest in the middle of the room. I don't remember us moving toward each other.

"Because you lied to me." I have no anger left in me, my reply is only a matter of fact.

"Well you know everything now. There's nothing more to lie about, my truths are all lying here in front of you." She gestures, as if to show them all over the floor.

"Good."

She bites her lip and I look down at her mouth. For some reason it's even more enticing than it was all the times before.

"Now what?" Her breath is a whisper across my face, and I answer by doing the only other thing there is left to do.

I kiss her.

mmy

STANDING THERE KISSING in the middle of the dimly lit living room, everything that we just argued about melts into nothingness. It's only Jake and Emmy in this moment. None of the bullshit that happened earlier with my brother, or Jake yelling and being angry at me for not telling him the truth about walking away from millions—none of that matters in this moment.

We've been dancing around each other for nearly two weeks now. I'm drawn to him even though we don't know each other very well. Now that he's made his move—or did I make the first move? No matter who moved first, this whole thing between us feels like it was inevitable from the start.

Jake's hands grip my hair as my arms wrap around behind his neck. The air swirling around us crackles and shifts as our kissing becomes less needy and more passionate. His hands fall away from my hair and slide down my back, stopping at my butt. He pulls me into him then hoists me up and, once again, I find myself wrapping my legs around his waist. Jake pulls back from kissing my swollen lips but not far.

"Bedroom or couch?" His lips cover mine again, giving me no chance to answer his question. I pull my hand from his hair and wave in the general direction of my room, too addicted to his mouth to be more specific. I nearly moan in relief that he understands my nonverbal command.

Without ever breaking our contact, he walks us in the direction of my room. Before we make it all the way into the bedroom, he lowers me back onto my feet. Leaning back into the doorframe, I stare up at him. His eyes are hooded, his lips puffy from my own. A brief pang of panic surges through my veins that maybe he's changed his mind. When his smile slowly drags across his face, the feeling evaporates immediately. He leans back into me, leaving only a millimeter of space between us. I can't look away from his heat-filled eyes as he closes the gap.

His hands find my hair again, gently tugging at it—a feeling I like all too much. I reach down and pull his shirt from his pants, fumbling with the buttons. It's not my finest moment when trying to undress a man, but I'm finding it hard to focus on the damn buttons while his tongue is dancing with mine.

Shit, why are there so many buttons?

The struggle is real, and he chuckles.

Finally freeing the last button, I slide my hands up his hot, bare chest, pushing his shirt away as he shrugs out of it. I admire him for a moment, standing there in only his slacks, then I reach for his belt buckle.

He shakes his head. "You need to catch up."

I pull off my denim jacket with incredible ease, all while watching him slowly undo his belt. Once he's unbuckled it, he pauses his progress and kisses me again.

Running my hands over the hard muscles of his arms and chest, I take in the soft but taut feel of his skin. My touch must trigger a shift as hands start roaming and kisses become more urgent.

Barely breaking the kiss, he reaches down and grabs the hem of my skirt in his fist. Pulling it up and over my head, the skirt and top coming off together, he leaves me in only my fleshy pink undies and matching strapless.

"You're so gorgeous, Emmy." His reverent voice is uneven as he takes me in.

This time when our lips meet, his hands also find my breasts.

My own hands clearly have a mind of their own as they drift down his body with a clear destination. Wasting no time, I pop the button and shove my hand down his pants, grabbing him firmly.

His kiss falters, his breathing catches, and he drops his head to my shoulder as I adjust my grip for a better hold. I pump up and down only a few times before he pulls away from me.

Smugness clouds his face as he picks me up again—this seems to be his thing —and carries me to my bed. In the few steps it takes to get us there, he has my bra unhooked. He lays me down with more finesse than I expected, pulling my strapless away from my body, tossing it on the floor.

He leans down with determined swiftness and lavishes my breast. I can't hold back the moan that escapes as it's been way too long since they've gotten any attention. Minutes later, he makes his way down my body, over my quivering stomach before finally stopping at my panty line.

He must sense me watching him because, as he stops, he looks up and grins. "I've thought about this moment many, many times."

"Oh yeah?" I blush at the thought of him having fantasies about me.

"Yes. I hope you don't mind if I take my time." His eyebrow quirks in challenge.

"When did you become such a gentleman?" I giggle.

"Baby, I've always been a gentleman." His smile is so bright when he winks that I nearly swoon instead of rolling my eyes. Cheesy lines have always been for the birds until now.

"Just get on with it. The suspense is killing me," I joke but I really may die if I have to wait any longer to feel that warm, attentive tongue of his.

With a smirk, he pulls my undies down my legs then tosses them on the floor with my bra.

True to his word, Jake takes his time with lazy kisses and drawn-,out licks. He pushes me to the edge only to pull me back, over and over again. A game that only he's playing, yet one I'm enjoying. Finally, he lets me break apart on his tongue.

Allowing me several gratifying breaths, he pushes up from the bed and pulls his wallet from his back pocket, grabbing a condom. He tosses his wallet on the nightstand nearby and steps out of his pants taking his briefs with them.

He's utterly magnificent and I'm speechless. All hard lines and smooth skin, yet soft to the touch. There isn't a single inch of him that isn't perfect. I'll have to spend more time in the gym to even the playing field a little.

I'm lost in my perusal of his flawless body when the sound of a rip of foil draws my eyes to the girth between his legs. He rolls on the condom then grins as he crawls up my body.

"You like what you see?" His voice is gruff.

I'm so ready for him that just the sound of his voice causes me to shiver. On autopilot, my hands lift to him and I run my fingertips over his now cooled skin. "Very much." My body is clearly acting on its own as my legs spread to make room for his hips. I bite my lip as I feel him line himself up with my center. My breath catches in my throat. I don't breathe again until he pushes into me and both of us are gasping for breath.

He feels so right. A perfect fit.

Moving together, we fall into a natural rhythm. A rhythm that is comfortable and familiar but at the same time also new and exciting. When I start seeing stars, he presses his mouth to mine, kissing me through my orgasm. The act draws out my pleasure as his body tenses over mine. He presses his forehead to my shoulder and finds his own release.

At that moment, I feel the need for him take root in my heart, in every way. Like his soul has merged with mine, this thing between us far from done.

The sounds of our heavy breaths fill the room as I slowly ease the grip I have on his back.

As I do, he leans up, looking down at me. His gives me a soft smile then leans in and kisses my nose. "That was ..." He trails off, maybe all his words were lost with my own.

"Amazing?" I offer.

He thinks about it, tapping his chin.

"The best sex you've ever had?" Trying again.

"Meh, it was alright." The jerk shrugs.

"Hey! Be nice!" I push at him as I fake pout, fighting back a giggle. He laughs and rolls us over and pulls me into his side.

"I was." He's still laughing as I snuggle into his side, resting my head on his shoulder.

He draws lazy circles over my naked shoulder, his other hand under his head.

"So, if Becca knows about the money, do your other friends?" He's casual, but I know there's something more in his tone.

"Becca's the only person from my old life that's not family who I'm still in contact with. As for my new friends, it's not that they don't know, but I've never talked to them about it. Besides the fact that I live here, I don't live like I have all the money in the world. Plus, I really don't have a lot of friends outside of work."

"Really?"

"Really. It's always been hard for me to make friends. To even date for that matter."

"Why's that?"

"Silly boy. Because of the stupid money." I dig a finger into his side. He reacts by twitching and grabbing my hand. Someone's ticklish.

"If money buys happiness, doesn't it buy friends?" He doesn't let go of my hand, but plasters it to his chest, covering it with his own.

I snort. "Money absolutely doesn't buy happiness if you're already lonely. When you live the high-society lifestyle, it's hard to find friends that are the real deal. I was lucky to find Bex at such a young age, but usually the friends you make in those kinds of social circles are really only friends by association."

"Uh." I can tell he's trying to wrap his head around my explanation.

"Remember that show from several years ago, *Gossip Girl?*" I hated the show, mostly because it was way too close to the life I was living and hated. No, I obsessed over shows like *Smallville* and *Gilmore Girls*. Shows from small towns that featured loving parents and supportive friends. Not absent parents and backstabbing socialites.

"Yeah, caught my brother, Kevin, watching it a few times." He chuckles.

"I bet you had fun with that." I smile, this conversation is so easy with him despite the topic.

"Hell yeah, I did."

"Well, that show ... that was what real life was like for me. Having a group of friends but knowing in a heartbeat that they'd all turn their back on you at any moment. You never know who your true friends are until the shit hits the fan."

"That doesn't sound like a great life."

"It isn't when you don't spend your days gossiping and spending Mommy and Daddy's money. Neither of those things interested me. Don't get me wrong, I love shopping. And I didn't mind having unlimited funds, but I also knew that I would give it up in a second if that meant that I could start making my own life decisions. What extracurricular activities to be involved in, what colleges I would apply to, even though one had already been chosen for me."

"I get it. You had the world at your fingertips, but it wasn't yours to do with how you pleased."

Yes, he finally does get it.

"Exactly. Once I hit eighteen, I started defying my dad's decisions. He was not happy with me going to Cornell, but I told him I'd find a way to pay for it myself or I wasn't going to any college. He couldn't have that. Whichever son of some high-profile businessman I ended up marrying someday would expect a well-educated housewife. So, I got my college of choice. When I graduated, I told my dad I was done living by his rules. It didn't go over well. It has been several years now and, as you can tell, things between my family and me aren't easy. But I'm happy and not having a lot of money suits me. I've come to appreciate things. I still love to shop, but I'm on a strict budget."

I chuckle to myself about how I'd really love a bigger clothes budget.

"You said dating is hard. Why?"

"I never know if a guy is into me because of my name and the money they think I have, or if they are into just me." Craig was the last guy I had a relationship with, but I've attempted to date since then. People recognize the King name and unless I change my name, I won't ever be able to escape the legacy.

"So, the fact that I clearly wasn't interested in you because you had money made things easy for you?" His tone is light, but I know I need to tread carefully.

I look up at him, to get a read on his expression. "My reputation couldn't be worse in the world I come from. If you weren't into me because of my money, then I knew you were safe." It's honest, and I hope it doesn't piss him off. He nods once, staring up at the ceiling, taking it all in.

After a few quiet moments, he asks, "Why didn't it work out with Craig?"

I sigh. Craig, oh Craig. "Craig's dad and mine were college roommates. To be clear, my father lived in the dorms only about six months before my grandfather bought him his first apartment. But Jerry and my dad stayed friends. I grew up with Craig. He's two years older than me, and we got along fine as kids. We weren't friends, yet we didn't dislike each other. Right before I graduated, my parents started pushing me to start dating, to get serious. Craig seemed like a well-adjusted adult, so if I had to date someone, I thought the fact that I already knew him was a good place to start.

"We dated for two years. We were together when I walked away from my family's money. He wasn't happy but I suspected that he didn't really care all that much. We never really loved each other. When he started pushing me to quit my job and start using my trust, I realized that he'd never support my need for independence, and that we were just wasting each other's time if we stayed together."

"He's a tool," Jake grumbles, sounding mad.

Suddenly I wonder if we've exceeded our after-sex cuddle and chat time. But he doesn't move away, his arm is still firmly wrapped around me. I stare off across the room unsure of what to say next. Until he speaks first.

"I think I needed you to be some rich trust-fund brat."

I suck in a breath, whispering my reply. "Why?"

"So, I wouldn't fall for you." His voice is low and gravelly.

"Because this whole thing between us is fake?" I brave asking it and I don't dare let out a breath, because I'm not sure I'll be able to handle his reply.

Shifting away from me slightly, he looks down at me. His eyes are filled with heat. "This isn't fake anymore, Emmy." There's no reassuring smile, no adoration in his eyes, I'm worried his words aren't meant to soothe me. That he's stating a fact and because of that, this realness between us can't continue.

I'm a bundle of confusion and dread. Staring into his eyes I'm unable to figure out what his words mean.

He must see my wheels turning because he visibly softens all the hard lines in his face. A small, sweet smile replaces his near frown. He pulls me to him and kisses my forehead. "It's late. Sleep." He resumes a lazy path over my shoulder and arm with his calloused fingers.

Minutes tick by and my eyes grow heavy. As I start to doze off, I feel him turn his head toward me and whispers into my hairline, "You're by far the best I've ever had."

I smile into the dark and fall asleep.

HOURS later when I blink open my eyes, I first notice the sun peeking through the blinds, which is most likely what woke me. I take a moment as the events of last night filter through my mind. I'm facing the opposite side from when I fell asleep, so I turn over to face Jake. But he isn't there. Sitting up, I look around my room. I lean over the bed to find his clothes are also missing.

Anxiety starts to flutter in my chest as I fear he left and didn't bother waking me. *Please just be in the kitchen or the bathroom.* I repeat this mantra in my head as I pull my thin cotton robe off the hook in my closet and slip into it, tying the sash as I step out of my room. The rest of the apartment is quiet. I don't have to strain my ears to know I'm most likely alone. I walk to the bathroom and see the door open, lights off. I walk back to my room to see if he at least left a note.

My heart has progressed from fluttering to pounding and I'm starting to worry I imagined last night. Maybe I just dreamed about having the best sex ever. Maybe Jake was so mad he didn't give me a chance to explain my life. Did I just write myself into an alternative ending?

Searching my room, there's nothing on the nightstand. I crawl onto my bed and move the sheets around, lift, and look under pillows. I won't admit this to a soul, but at one point I desperately crawl on the floor around my bed in hopes of finding a fallen note.

Nothing.

He's just gone.

Chewing on my lip, I realize I have no idea where my phone is. I never saw it in my pursuit for a note. Thankfully, it's still in my purse, which I put on the table last night when we got back after the party.

I hurry back out to the table and fish out my phone. There is a text from Becca, and two missed calls as well as a text from Levi, all from this morning. I realize that it's a little past nine. Then I see it.

A hastily scribbled note from Jake next to my purse. My eyes blur while I quickly try to read it. I slam my eyes shut to focus myself before reopening them and carefully reading his note.

Sex with you was everything I had hoped it would be and more. But that's all it was, and it won't happen again.

He even signed it "Jake Harper," as if I wouldn't know who left the note. And then it hits me, I hardly knew anything about him. This fake relationship was so focused on me and my family and him getting his money that we never really got to know one another, aside from the moments when we were faking it. I just had amazing passionate sex with a man who didn't even think I knew his last name. Was he making a point that I don't know enough about him? If that was the case, maybe he shouldn't have given me two orgasms before he left me in the middle of the night.

Heart, meet fist.

ake

I'M A JACKASS.

I'll admit it to myself, that sneaking out on Emmy early this morning was a jackass move.

But I did it, there's no changing it. The letter I left her—that ... well, that was a dick move. But I don't have a time machine, so I have to admit that I'm a jackass dick and move on. Because moving on is what needs to happen.

When I got home around three this morning, I tossed and turned until eight trying to get some sleep. I've been sulking around my shitty apartment all morning. I'm grumpy and tired. It's nearly one and I'm lounging on the couch, waiting for Kevin to arrive. He's coming over to watch the Mets since they are at an away game today.

My phone rings and I steel myself before picking it up off the coffee table. Emmy. This is the first I've heard from her today. I'm tempted to answer, staring at her name on my screen. A pounding comes at my front door. Kevin is here. My decision is made for me and I set down the phone and get up to let him in.

"Yo." He hurries in past me. "Sorry I'm late, the subway was packed today."

"I was wondering if you were going to miss the opening pitch." I lock up behind him.

Kevin quickly makes himself at home by grabbing a beer out of the fridge, a jar of salsa, and a bag of chips from the counter. Hands full, he deposits it all onto the coffee table. He must have grabbed the opener because he uses it to open his beer then twists open the brand-new jar of salsa with a pop. As he rips into the bag of chips, he says, "Dude, the game's starting, are you gonna sit?" Then he shoves a few chips into his mouth.

"Make yourself at home, Kev," I mutter as I grab myself a beer.

As I sit down next to him, my phone alerts me to a voicemail. My god, that's either a long-ass message or I missed the first alert.

Kevin notices and looks down at my phone but then focuses back on the game.

I snag up my phone and shove it in my pocket.

He lets it go for a few minutes, longer than I expected.

"So, how's that going? Your fake girlfriend?" he asks between mouthfuls of salsa-covered chips.

I grunt.

"That great, huh? Is she a total bitch?"

"Watch it," I nearly growl.

He pulls his eyes from the television and leans away from me. "Duuude. What? We haven't talked about it in a while. I thought you said she was some stuck-up rich chick."

I shake myself out of it, he doesn't deserve my foul mood. "No, it's fine. It's just, she isn't a bitch."

He eyes me before shrugging a nonverbal "alright" and turning back to the game.

"So, things are good or bad with her, Emmy, right?" He keeps his focus on the game.

"Emmy." Just saying her name makes my body heat up with thoughts of last night. Shit, last night, the sex was so fucking good. "No, things are over with her."

"Huh." He cocks his head, giving me the side-eye.

I'm leaning back into the couch with my arms crossed.

The broadcast jumps into its first commercial break. Kevin faces me, studying me while he drinks his beer, slowly. I ignore him. He doesn't let up. I press my lips together and then chew on the inside of my cheek to keep from engaging him.

I can feel his stare and it's really starting to grate on my nerves.

"Oh my god, what?" I snap.

"Nothing." He shrugs and turns back to the television.

"What do you mean nothing? You're giving me the look, and I don't appreciate it." I twist my upper body to face him.

"What look?"

"*The* look. You know, the one Mom gave us growing up when she wanted us to spill our guts."

He nods in acknowledgement. "Oh, that one. Yeah, I'm familiar." He dunks a chip in the jar of salsa. I just stare at him. "You know, now that you mention it, you do seem like you need to get something off your chest. So, what's up?"

I glare at him.

"What's going on with Emmy that has your panties in such a twist?"

"She's been lying to me," I grunt.

"Shit, man, about what?" He's giving me his full attention, the little punk pulled one over on me.

"About the fact that she has no money." His eyebrows shoot straight up so I correct myself, "As in, she isn't rich. She has money, she works and pays her bills, but she's just solid middle class."

"How does she not have money? Isn't her dad some rich fuck who plays with makeup?"

I roll my eyes. Clearly, he only listens to half of what I say. "No, he runs and owns King Cosmetics. And she walked away from it. A few years ago. She wanted to live her own life, one without the expectations and duties that come with having that kind of cash."

"Wow. That had to be tough," he mutters into his beer.

I nod, staring at the game, not really seeing anything.

"She just told you and you ended things?"

"Kinda. We fought about it. Fucked, then I left." I'm not paying attention to the game or anything around me for that matter, but I hear the thump of his beer bottle on the coffee table. Tearing my gaze away from the TV, I look over at him. His eyes are wide and his mouth agape.

"What?"

"Do you hear yourself right now? When did you become an asshole?" I let out a humorless laugh.

Apparently, this morning.

"Please tell me you didn't leave without talking to her first. You didn't ghost her." He reads my silence and shakes his head.

"Oh, save it. I know it was a dick move."

"What the hell happened, man?"

"I was lying there, holding her next to me as she slept, and thinking about how she was the best sex I've ever had. That being with her, both between the sheets and not, just feels different. Like something more, something I've never felt with another woman." If I'm being honest, the thoughts nearly wrecked me. I couldn't believe just how right she actually felt.

"So, what's the issue?" The game completely lost to us both now.

"While I was thinking all this stuff, I remembered where I was. I was lying there in a big comfy bed on the fourteenth floor of 425 Madison." He starts to speak, I know to bring up my residents rule, but that wasn't the issue. "No, I realized that I didn't belong in that bed. I didn't belong in that room. The only reason I should be in those apartments is to fix all the shit those rich fucks can't fix themselves." My body began to shake. "Even though Emmy works hard at her job, to make a life for herself, she's still rich. She might not have millions in some bank account, but at any minute she could change that. She might be semi-estranged from her family but that doesn't change the fact that they will always push her to come back, to take what is rightfully hers and be who they expect her to be. And who that is, is a millionaire."

Kevin shakes his head, clearly confused. He stands, pauses, shakes his head again, then continues on into the tiny kitchen nook. "I can't believe all the shit that just spewed from your mouth."

I roll my eyes.

"I don't know when you became so jaded, but this is not you. You're being downright ridiculous about this. That shit you pulled sneaking out on her, I'm just..." He trails off, looking shocked as he stands in front of the fridge.

"You're just what?" I don't know that I want him to finish the sentence.

"I'm just disappointed in you." He lifts a shoulder and walks back to the couch.

"Disappointed? Oh, get over yourself. Why the hell are *you* disappointed? You don't even know Emmy, she's just another chick to you. What do you care?"

"I care because you're my brother. I care because you clearly have feelings for this woman. I care because my big brother is suddenly a coward."

"I'm not a coward." I'm such a fucking coward but I'm still in the mood to fight.

"You are! You're too scared to admit to yourself and her how you feel. Man up, Jake." Not only am I getting my ass chewed by my little brother, I'm missing my team play.

"I'm not scared."

"Well then, what are you?" he challenges.

"I'm a maintenance man for Christ's sake!" I lose my cool now and jump up from the couch like it's on fire.

"I know what you do for a living. What's the problem?" He's back to shoveling the fucking chips into his mouth now. Did he not freaking eat today?

"No woman—especially one like Emmy—would ever be content marrying a maintenance man." My hands dig through my hair and I'm close to ripping it out.

"Jake, that's not your decision to make."

I scoff.

"I'm sure Emmy would love the opportunity to make her own decision when it comes to who she marries. Yeah? Sound familiar?" He sits back with a smug-ass look on his face. "I mean, think about it, Jake. She did walk away from millions so she could live her own life, to make decisions on her own."

"It's not the same." I turn my back to him.

"Have you thought about the fact that maybe you're the one who's insecure about your career?" He has my attention again, but if looks could kill, he'd be six feet under right now. He continues, "What if no matter who you're with, you'll never feel equal in your relationship. Maybe it's not them, it's you."

I haven't punched him in more than a decade. I don't know if it's acceptable to beat the shit out of your little brother at nearly thirty, but I'm thinking that it should be my brotherly right no matter what age I am. All the shit he's spouting is just that ... shit.

"Whatever, man." I shake my head.

"The sooner you can admit it to yourself, the sooner you'll be happy."

"I am happy."

He laughs at this. "You are not happy, brother. Not at all."

"Whatever," I grumble again.

He casually turns back to the television, focusing back on the game. As he reaches for the remote, I assume to turn up the volume, he lands one more blow to my newly bruised ego. "It's your life to fuck up. It's no sweat off my sack. Emmy should be relieved not to be dragged down into your pit of self-pity and insecurity."

The heat in my veins starts to boil. I ball my fists and shove them in my front pockets. I bite the inside of my cheek to keep from letting all the words filtering though my head explode out of my mouth. Turning my back, I walk as calmly as I can to the bathroom.

I will not hit my brother.

I will not hit my brother.

I repeat the phrase over and over. Gripping the bathroom counter, I hang my head and breathe deep, yet shaky breaths as I count to ten. Then I splash water over my face and dry it off with the towel hanging nearby. I shake the frustration out with a full-body shake starting from my head, to my shoulders, and then arms.

I walk back into the living room and find him engrossed in the game.

"We are done with this conversation. You can either shut up about it and watch the game or get the fuck out." I don't sit down just yet, I need to hear his answer first. I'll either grab another beer or I'll be slamming the door as he leaves.

He gives me side-eye and pretends to think about it. I cross my arms. "Well?"

"Well, the beer is free here, so I'll shut up and stay."

I nod and grab another beer.

Kevin ended up staying about an hour after the game ended. I ordered a pizza, and he ate half of it. After the ultimatum I gave him, he did shut up about Emmy and that bullshit about being insecure. We were actually able to enjoy the rest of the game. It was a good one, too. The Mets won by three.

Now, as I sit here on my bed getting ready to turn in for the night, I stare down at my phone. My home screen still shows a missed call and voicemail. I'm drawn to her name on my screen. I want to listen to the voicemail, but I need to think everything through.

I think about all the shit Kev spouted off about today.

Maybe I am insecure. I love what I do, but it doesn't mean I'm not worried about finding someone who's okay with being with someone who is just a simple man living a blue-collar life, as I'll never make the big bucks.

I might have grown up in a single-parent household. One where my mom worked two jobs at one point. I always told myself that someday when I was married and had kids, I would support my family. I would do everything in my power to make sure my wife was happy and had everything she needed. Maybe because my mom didn't have the same opportunity, I wanted to be able to give my wife the option of not having to work if that was her choice. That mentality was stuck in my brain before I realized that being a handyman was my calling. It's been hard to align my truth with my somewhat stunted belief of who should be the breadwinner in a family.

Truth is, Emmy will always have more than me. What could I ever give her that she doesn't already have access to?

Nothing.

That thought nearly breaks me.

In the end, I open my voicemail screen and delete her message.

It's probably for the best, anyway.

CHAPTER 17

I ROLL the faux-wooden ball down the lane with so much force I'm slightly worried the ball is going to break something. Thankfully, it doesn't. It sinks into the right-hand five hundred hole, resulting in a nearly perfect game. I can't say that I'm enjoying myself, but I needed to blow off some steam. Since I'm not a runner, I thought a nice round, or ten, of Skee-Ball would work. I know, the two aren't really comparable, but I've got a Skee-Ball machine in my apartment. Who wouldn't opt for a few rounds?

I've got music pumping through one of our voice-enabled speakers, but the combination of my favorite mix and my favorite arcade game doesn't seem to be helping my mood.

It's been three days since I woke up in my bed sans Jake. I'm throwing around a lot of anger at what happened. Anger is better than sadness though, which is something I'm also struggling with. Every time I start to feel sad, I just get pissed. I'm a roller coaster of emotions. Hence the force behind my Skee-Ball game.

I'm miffed because I opened up to Jake. I told him everything. There is only one other person in the world who knows all my issues and I currently live with her. I know Jake wouldn't be able to fully understand my life and how it was and why I walked away, but it felt like he was accepting of it. That he was able to understand my choices. I'm also mad because of the sex.

We had amazing sex and our chemistry was through the roof. We'd been dancing around all that sexual tension for a couple weeks and once we made fireworks, he bolted.

Here's where the sadness comes in. I feel like I lost someone, someone extremely important to me. Sure, it's only been a couple weeks, but we got to know each other. We had gotten used to each other; I came to rely on him. Now he's gone. There's a clear void there. It's like, as quickly he took up residence in my heart, he vanished just as fast.

Then I just start to feel stupid. Stupid me, for thinking we were anything more than what we were. We were never supposed to be real. I should have stayed strong, fought the pull. Feeling embarrassed about my stupidity just makes me mad all over again.

I turn off the machine, done with my attempt to roll away my anger, just as Becca walks through the front door.

"Guess what?" she yells over my music, walking into the kitchen. There's a brown paper bag in her arm. If I were to guess, she's brought us food.

"What?" I eye her but throw myself onto the couch.

"Today is the day you get over Jake Harper and move on." She busies herself by taking things out of the bag.

I cross my arms and glare at her.

She tells the speaker to turn off the music before replying, "You've been angry with a side of mopey for three days now over a fake relationship. It's time to move on and I've brought in reinforcements."

I don't reply but increase my glare level.

She lifts the makings of a grilled cheese up for me to see and then waves around a pint of Phish Food ice cream. My attitude toward my bestie simmers just a bit.

"What kind of cheese did you get?" My tone is challenging.

"American, right from the deli, as well as cheddar and pepper jack. I figured you'd have two."

Dang. She passed my grilled cheese test, so I can't accuse her of making matters worse by making me talk about my failed fake relationship woes, when she's gotten my favorite combo of melty cheese.

"So how do you propose I get over the maintenance man ... today?" I might be a little less grouchy knowing there's cheesy goodness in my near future, but I'm in no way cured.

"Well, we will start by making a god-awful number of grilled cheese sandwiches. When we are done, we will eat ice cream and then about halfway through the pint, I will deliver you a kick-ass pep talk, and tomorrow when you wake up, you'll be good as new. Ready to face the world with one less chip on that dainty little shoulder of yours." She seems so sure of her plan.

I eye her skeptically but decide to throw her a bone. So, I get up and trade my seat on the couch for the stool at the bar area. Sliding onto the high stool, I tell her, "I don't like being grouchy."

"Aww, I don't like you being grouchy, either." She smiles as she gets to work on the sandwiches.

"Just give me the pep talk now so I don't have to think about it while I eat my carbs."

"Okay, good, because I didn't think I was going to be able to wait."

I roll my eyes at her confession.

"I know you feel like an idiot. You had a fake relationship with him and so you feel stupid for thinking it was more than that. But you shouldn't because I think it would have happened to anyone. I mean, hello, Debra Messing totally fell for her man whore in *The Wedding Date*." I snort. She continues, "Point is, you felt more than he did. That's okay. Like seventy percent of relationships end because someone loved the other more."

"I didn't say anything about love. And I can't help feel like you just made up that percentage."

She hand-waves my remark. "Like sixty-five percent of statistics are made up anyway. I was making a point."

I stare at her, trying to process what she just said, when she gives me a sly smile.

"Anyway, it happened and now it's over. Time to move on. Look at it this way, you had some much-needed sex."

She has a point, I did need some really great sex.

She places the buttered bread on the skillet and my stomach rumbles.

"You are a strong, independent woman. You move on and find someone who wants all of you and your crazy. I promise you, it will happen."

"I hear what you are saying, I know you are right. I just feel like I didn't get any closure."

"Closure on what? A fake relationship?" she challenges.

"I guess, but I swear, it didn't feel fake anymore."

"Then get closure." She slides a spatula under the first sandwich to check the toastiness of the bread.

"Yeah, I'm pretty sure that message you left him isn't going to help me get said closure."

She sniffs. "Whatever. I was mad, and you had tear-stained cheeks and bloodshot eyes when I got home Sunday afternoon. I needed to get something off my chest."

"Yeah, well, maybe he didn't listen to the message." I really hope he didn't listen. Bex wasn't nice. Something about his little dick and knowing people who could make his life hell. She won't go through with any of those mindless threats, but it probably pushed us both farther into the crazy-zone.

"So, you haven't heard from him?" Her tone is more sympathetic now.

"Not a word. I haven't even seen him around the building."

She harrumphs in reply.

We are quiet for a while until she pulls the first grilled cheese off the heat and plates it.

"I'll gladly make you more if you need them," she offers, handing the plate to me.

"Surely you don't think I can eat four of these?" I laugh.

"No, silly. Two are for me."

We eat our grilled cheeses and then ice cream. We don't bring up Jake again, opting instead to watch whatever popular competition show is currently airing on network television for a couple hours.

It's about eight and I'm contemplating just going to bed. If I'm going to wake up without the fake-Jake chip on my shoulder tomorrow, I might as well give myself extra wallowing time in my bed.

I hear a knock at the door. I glance at Becca and she eyes the door. My heart rate quickens, and she pushes off the couch to answer it. She looks through the peephole, and her shoulders sag in relief.

"It's your brother," she says and then swings the door open.

"To what do we owe the pleasure of this visit, Mr. King?" Becca snips. She's known Levi as long as she's known me. In high school, I thought that she might have had a crush on him. But to my knowledge nothing ever came of it. They've never not gotten along, but she's always been on my side. She knows he is the cause of Jake finding out about my money. Or lack thereof.

He looks startled at her snip but walks into the apartment anyway. "I need to talk to Emmy."

Closing the door behind him, she mutters under her breath, "Clearly, as you wouldn't be here to see me."

"Emmy, you haven't returned my calls or my texts." He seems annoyed.

"Yeah, well, I'm mad at you." I cross my arms.

"What the hell for?" He stops mid-step and stares at me.

I cock my head and give him a "think about it" look.

Realization dawns on him. "Oh, for causing that rift between you and Jake?" He has the good grace to look ashamed. "I'm sorry about that, I hope I didn't cause too much of an issue for you." He continues to the couch and sits down beside me.

Becca snorts, shakes her head and tells us she'll be in her room.

I ignore his comment, not really wanting to get into a thing about Jake right now. Turning to him, I ask, "So tell me why you're here. You never visit me."

He sighs and leans back, resting his head on the back of the couch as he closes his eyes. "I called off the engagement."

"Shut the front door."

"True story, bro." He still has his eyes closed.

"Why haven't I heard about this yet?"

"Well, for starters, you haven't picked up your phone when I call." He pops open an eye and glares at me.

"Sorry, I've been preoccupied. I haven't even heard from Kitty yet." Not that I would want to, she'd blame me for this, no matter Levi's reasons.

"Neither have I."

"I'm not saying that I'm happy you did it, but I can't say that I'm disappointed either. Whatever your reason, I'm proud that you did something." I pat his arm. We aren't a very touchy-feely family, so while most sisters would use this moment to hug their big brothers, I settle on an arm pat.

Levi chuckles in return and covers my hand on his arm, squeezing it lightly. "Thanks, Ems."

"Are you going to tell me why you called things off with Darcy?" I slowly pull my hand away. Twisting toward him, I lift my legging-covered legs onto the couch and tuck them under me.

"The long and short of it was that you were right."

"Wait," I interject. "What was that?"

"Har har, you heard me."

"I may have possibly misheard you. It sounded like you said I was right." I feign concern.

He smiles and looks at me. "You heard correctly. Anyway, I decided I'd rather be single than marry someone I'm not in love with. Not to mention someone who is an eager fucking beaver, ready to cheat before we even say our vows."

I give him a wan smile. "You deserve so much more than that, Levi."

"I know. Thank you for pushing me on it."

"Anytime, big bro. As your little sister, I take my duty of telling you when you're wrong very seriously. You can always count on me." I salute him.

He chuckles.

"So, what are the ramifications of this whole thing? Surely Dad isn't happy. Kitty is probably shitting a brick." I shake off the visual.

"You're probably right on both accounts, but I haven't spoken to either of them yet. I just called things off with Darcy late last night. I took the day off to avoid Dad."

"You took a day off?" I perk up in my seat, cock an eyebrow, and start looking over him. Checking his face, looking at the clothes he's wearing. I lean over and look down at his shoes. He scoffs.

"You *look* like Levi. But the Levi I know doesn't take time off. Are you sick? Do I need to take you to the doctor?"

He reaches out and covers my face with his hand, pushing me away. He's always done this to me. So, I do the only thing I've ever done back. I lick his palm.

"Ew. You're gross." He pulls his hand away and wipes it on his pant leg.

I smirk.

"Ems, you have no room to talk. You're just as much a workaholic as Dad and me. Where do you think you got it from?" He has a point, but I shrug it off.

"So, what do you think Dad will do?"

Levi sighs heavily. "I don't know. I doubt he fires me. Worst-case scenario, I lose my trust."

"What? How? You're thirty-one. You've been drawing on that thing for six years. You can't just lose it. Can you?"

"Well, since Dad is the trustee on it, he can always change the rules of it. He was very, very adamant about me marrying. When I was unable to find any prospects, he pushed Darcy my way. Well, Kitty did."

"I think that's stupid. But I doubt you lose your trust. Maybe you'll just be the black sheep for a little while." I smile ruefully. "Maybe taking the heat off me for a bit? Eh?"

"Doubt it. As long as you refuse the family money, you'll always be the black sheep. But I'll see what I can do." He's always looked out for me.

"Thanks, big brother."

"So, you want to tell me about that whole mess with Jake?" He's apparently done talking about his issues.

My turn to sigh, I pull off the Band-Aid. "As you guessed the other night, I hired Jake to be my boyfriend for the duration of the wedding events. The whole mess came about when you spilled the beans about how I had no money."

"I suspected there was something fishy between the two of you, but never expected you'd hire a boyfriend. Jesus, Emmy." While he looks confused, he doesn't look disgusted with me. That's a plus.

"I know, it's one of the crazier things I've done."

"Yeah, right up there with walking away from a multimillion-dollar trust fund." He snorts.

I just nod, defeated.

"So, you hire this guy to be your fake date and tell him you're going to pay him when you don't have any money? So, this whole thing is about money?"

"Kinda."

"Then I say good riddance, if he's all up in arms about money, he isn't worth it. Be glad it's fake."

My shoulders sag. "I said it was kind of about the money. Mostly, it was because I lied to him about having the money. I let him think I had it all, and he didn't much like being lied to."

Levi studies me for a few moments.

I focus on my fingers in my lap, picking at my nails.

"So, this wasn't fake, was it?" His tone is soft and concerned.

"No, I don't think so. I think we both started to have feelings for each other. So, the fact that I lied about not being rich made things feel fake again." My eyes remain focused on my lap.

"Well, does he want you to have money or *not* have money?" Levi reaches out and grabs my hands, stopping me from ruining my home-done manicure.

I lift my face to him. "I think he feels relieved that I don't have all that money, but he still doesn't think we are meant to be, so he's done." I don't tell him that Jake snuck out after sex. That's just not something you tell your brother. Levi squeezes my hands before letting them go.

"So, I have to ask. How much are you supposed to pay him?"

I mumble the amount, looking back down at my hands.

"I'm sorry, you're going to have to speak up."

"I said fifteen thousand."

"What? Are you shitting me right now?" He's leaning toward me now, wide-eyed with shock.

"No, I'm not. But now that there's no more wedding, I need to pay up. Unfortunately, I don't have the money yet. I was due for a bonus next month. Combine that with what I have in savings and I'd have just enough to pay him."

"Paying him now means you don't have the money." Levi sighs in understanding.

"Bingo." I offer him a sad smile.

"Shit, little sister. How did you get yourself into this mess? You're telling me a fake date was worth fifteen grand all for what? A few dates around the family?"

"It was Becca's idea," I offer, but it doesn't matter. I went through with it.

He rolls his eyes as I continue, "I wasn't going to do it until I started getting calls from Craig about wanting to get back together."

"What is it that Becca calls him? Cringey Craig? I mean, he's never been my favorite guy either, but ..." He finishes his sentence with a whistle.

After a few beats, he speaks.

"I'm going to give you the money. It's the least I can do. One, for causing issues between the two of you the other night. Two, I still feel like shit for what I said about you paying him with sex. And three, I called off the wedding, therefore ushering in the need for you to have the money sooner than expected." He leans over a little and fishes his phone out of his side pocket.

"No way. I'm not going to take money from you. This is my bed, now let me lie in it." I shake my head furiously.

"Let me loan it to you then. Family interest rate of: pay it back when you can and not in one lump sum."

"Levi, really, no." My eyes water because he's always looked out for me, but he isn't paying attention as he's doing something on his phone.

"Done, too late. I've just transferred the money. You should be good to write him a check tomorrow."

I fling my arms around him and hug him this time, telling him thank you. He chuckles and hugs me back.

A COUPLE DAYS LATER, I have a check in hand, for fifteen grand made out to Jake. I stand in the middle of my apartment staring at the small piece of paper, wondering how to get it to him. I don't have his address, so I can't mail it to him. I texted him this morning and surprise, surprise, he never replied. I can't say that the fact that he is ignoring me is helping my confidence levels. When you sleep with a guy and he goes MIA, it's hard to feel good about yourself. Not to mention, my heart is just a bit numb. I was falling for Jake. Those feelings, I thought, were mutual.

Anyway, I don't want to have a face-to-face with him, but I need to pull up my big-girl panties and get it over with. Decision made, I fold the check, put it in my pocket and head down to the maintenance office.

Minutes later, once I'm standing outside the office, I take a deep breath.

You can do it.

I push the door open and step inside.

A man I've seen around the building before, stands inside, leaning over the desk and looking through a pile of paper. He lifts his head and smiles kindly at me. He's older than me, maybe by ten years, and his sharp, expensive suit tells me he comes from money.

"Can I help you?"

"Yeah, I was looking for Jake."

"He's off today. I'm Leo, I own this building. Is there anything I can do for you?" He puts the papers down and extends a hand for me to shake.

"Emmy. And no, I needed to talk to him for a minute that's all. I'll catch up with him later." I smile. "Thank you, though." I offer a small wave as he nods and goes back to the papers on the desk.

I leave the office and walk back out to the lobby.

Think, think.

I want to get this over with. Then I decide that I at least attempted to woman-up for a face-to-face, it's not my fault he wasn't around. So, I walk to the concierge desk.

"Hey, Lisa." I smile as I come to a stop at the desk.

"Hi, Emmy. How can I help you this evening?" She's the second-shift concierge. She's about twenty-five and as sweet as can be.

"I'm fine. Do you have an envelope I can use?"

"Of course." She leans down to open one of the drawers behind the counter and pulls out a crisp white envelope. I thank her as she hands it to me.

I pull the check out and put it in the envelope, lick the back and close it. Then I grab a 425 Madison-branded pen from a holder on the counter and write Jake's name on the front of the envelope.

"Where can I put this to make sure he gets it?" I lift it up showing her the name. "It's very important."

"He has a mailbox. And don't worry, it's locked and only he has the key, so it's safe too."

"That's perfect." I take a relaxing breath. I wasn't feeling great about leaving a fifteen-thousand-dollar check at the desk, but I've made worse choices.

"It's box 104." She nods toward the mail room.

With a thanks, I turn and walk to the boxes. Finding 104, I slip it right into the box. I wipe my hands on my pants and head back upstairs.

I guess I can now consider this business transaction closed. Which is the only way I can think about it.

I will not cry.

CHAPTER 18

 ake

I'm still a jackass.

I've still not faced Emmy. I haven't texted her or called her. She texted me a couple days ago. She said she needed to talk to me, but I let the message go unanswered.

I'm not this guy. The guy who sneaks out on a girl after sex. I'm not the kind of guy who doesn't text back.

I'm not the kind of guy who does this to a woman he actually likes.

I really fucking like Emmy.

This past week without talking to her, seeing her, hearing her voice, it's made me realize just how much I do like her. I fucking miss her.

Everything Kevin laid out on the floor for me during the ball game has been stirring around in my brain this past week. I've thrown myself into work, surprise, surprise. Even on my day off, I ended up coming in and covering a shift for Mel, one of the other guys on the team.

Needless to say, I've been thinking about my own issues and insecurities on repeat.

I was hoping I'd see her at some point this week though. In the lobby, near the elevators, even up on her floor. I haven't been hiding, but I haven't gone out of my way to seek her out.

I know I could just call her or text her, but I'm a shit and my avoidance skills are in high form right now. I need to apologize, at least.

I've got maybe two hours left of my shift and I'm dragging my feet. I wander out in the lobby, for no other reason than I hope to see Emmy on her way home for the day.

I'm just entering the lobby when Lisa, the evening concierge, waves me over. She's young and attractive, but you know my rule. It goes for co-workers too.

"Hey, Lisa, what's up?" I nod.

"Not much, ready for the weekend. Are you here tomorrow or do you have Saturday off?"

"I'm actually not back on until Sunday night, then I'm here all week."

"Well enjoy your Saturday and Sunday." She's a sweet kid. Okay, she isn't a kid, twenty-five or so. Around Kev's age. I still think of him as a kid.

I tap the counter and start to continue my way out of the building when she stops me. "Oh, did you get Emmy's letter?"

I stop and turn my head toward her.

"Yeah, she had something for you a couple days ago. She put it in your mailbox. It looked important."

Shit. That damn mailbox.

"No, I didn't. Thanks for letting me know, Lisa." I spin on my heel and nearly run to the mail room. It's not a room per se, but more like a nook, that houses all the mailboxes on a single wall. Each mailbox has a letter-sized slot for easy distribution. I don't know why, but every employee has a box. I never check mine, it's not as if I ever get mail here. Fortunately, I keep my mail key on my key ring and pop it open.

Sure enough, there is a single envelope sitting there, waiting for me. I pull it out and close the box. Carefully, I rip open the envelope and pull out a check. A fucking check for fifteen grand made out to me. Signed by Emmy King herself.

Shit.

The pit of my stomach just drops.

I can't believe I'm holding a check for fifteen grand. I can't believe that she paid me even after what happened, especially since the wedding hasn't even happened yet.

If I didn't feel like shit before, I definitely do now.

I don't want her money—not after what occurred, that's for sure. Plus, I know she can't truly afford this.

Forgetting about the fact that I'm working, I walk to the elevators. Stepping in the car, I punch the number fourteen and impatiently push the button to close the door. Several times.

Suddenly I find myself knocking on Emmy's door. But it's not Emmy who answers.

"Oh, what do you want?" Becca sounds annoyed. I get it, I deserve her snark.

"Is Emmy here?" I try to look around her, but she blocks my view into the room.

"Nope." She pops the word.

I furrow my brow. "Look," I start in, but she holds a hand up.

"No, you look. Ghosting her after sex, that's shitty. But not letting her know that you've gotten her fifteen-thousand-dollar check, now that's fucked up."

I shake my head. "Yeah, I know, but I just got the check, like less than five minutes ago."

She eyes me, unsure if she should believe me or not.

"Can you just tell her I was here and need to talk to her?" I can't help the pleading tone of my voice.

"Here's an idea, buddy. Pick up the phone and call her. Call. Her."

I wouldn't say Becca shuts the door in my face at that point, but it's not a quiet "I live in an apartment and should be mindful of my neighbors" kind of shut.

With a sigh, I head back down to the lobby.

Once I'm back in the maintenance office, I pull out my phone and call her. The phone rings a few times, then I'm sent to voicemail. Her adorably chipper voice makes me smile. I hang up at the beep. No, what I need to tell her has got to be face-to-face. Preferably in private.

About two hours later, I clock out for the day. I'm considering heading over to Monterey's for a drink before I head home. Normally, after a week like this, I'd open up Match Me and find a hookup for the night. But none of that interests me. I've actually considered deleting the app, but the timing might be immature. I'm just not feeling it, but that doesn't mean I should delete it.

I lock the office door behind me. It's only seven, but it's officially considered after hours. Mel is on tonight and he's already in the maintenance apartment for the night. It's not a bad gig, being on call here at 425 Madison. The tiny one-bedroom is decked out to the nines, making your night away from home while you work as comfortable as possible.

I barely clear the hall into the lobby when I see Emmy ahead of me, making her way toward the front of the building. I hurry to catch up. I push through the massive chrome doors and yell out to her.

"Emmy, wait!"

She stops and turns toward me. She looks a little startled at first, but she quickly replaces that look with disdain. Clearly, she isn't happy to see me. I'm not surprised. As I catch up to her, I notice how amazing she looks. She's dressed in tan dress pants and a silky, black, sleeveless top. She's wearing heels, which adds to her height and complements her already long, lean legs. When she doesn't have heels on, she tucks right up under my chin. At this height, though, I don't have to bend as far down to kiss her. Which is immediately what I start thinking about. Those pouty lips steal my focus, but I quickly regain it and look at the rest of her beautiful face.

"What do you want, Jake?" She crosses her arms.

Damn, her attitude is cute. I bite back a smile. "I don't want the check." I fish it out of my back pocket and hand it to her.

She looks down at what I'm offering, her eyes drawn, and brow furrowed.

"What do you mean you don't want it? We had a deal." She looks back up at me.

"I know, but I don't want it." I shake it toward her again, but she doesn't take it. Her face starts to blush. She shyly looks around and takes a step closer to me.

"Look, I'm good for it, I don't go back on my deals. And I don't appreciate you taking pity on me after what I told you last weekend." Her whisper is harsh.

She's embarrassed, and she thinks I don't want her money because I don't think she can afford it.

I shake my head. "One, I know you're good for it. Two, this isn't a pity thing. Promise." This seems to calm her a little.

"Then, what is it?"

"It's more like, I can't accept it." She opens her mouth, I'm sure to ask why, but I keep talking, "I broke the rules. Therefore, our deal is null and void."

She crosses her arms again. "What, the no-fucking-the-residents rule? You're an ass, Jake."

I chuckle, "Yes, I know I am."

Apparently, this pisses her off enough that she turns on her shiny, black heel and starts to walk away. But I reach out just in time and grab her arm.

"Wait, Emmy. Please." I try not to beg, but I'm nearing the point that I probably need to.

She huffs but turns to face me.

"I said *rules*, that was only one of the rules I broke." I can tell she's trying to recall them, there were only four: three of mine, one of hers.

"There was a fifth rule, an unspoken one. A rule I had for myself. That was to not fall for the gorgeous brunette who lives in unit fourteen-twelve." She gives me a sideways look, but her posture relaxes.

"I don't deserve this check. I don't want it. It's not what I want."

"What is it that you want, Jake?"

"You." It's all that needs said. She rolls her eyes, which is not what I was expecting.

"You left after sex. You wrote me a shitty letter."

"That I did, and I've regretted it every day since."

"Then why haven't you texted me? Or called me. You're clearly very skilled at ghosting people."

"I know, which is why I agreed with you about being an asshole." I can't help laughing.

"So, what's your excuse then?"

"I've had a really hard time getting past the fact that on paper, you and I don't make sense."

"What paper? There's no paper, Jake. It's just me and you." She doesn't seem to have much anger left, like she's lost her steam.

"I know, but the truth is you'll always be out of my league. You'll always have money, you were born into it. Even if you choose not to use it, it's still there. Tucked away safely, waiting for you when you decide to use it. But me, I've never had money, and I never will. Sometimes, it feels like I live paycheck to paycheck. I will always be a blue-collar worker."

She bites her lip while she tries to process everything I've laid out for her.

"I thought I was always content and secure in my career path. It always felt like what I was supposed to do. But after a few bad dates and not so wonderful ex-girlfriends, I realized that at some point down the line, I'd probably never make enough money to keep a wife happy, at least not when it comes to stability."

She puts up a hand to stop my admissions. "Jake, those bad dates, stupid ex-girlfriends, they aren't me. I walked away from millions so I could live my life the way I wanted to. I told you everything. I told you how money was of little importance to me. And you still didn't think I could handle you not making a lot of money? I thought you understood me. I know we've not known each other a long time, but I thought you knew me better than that."

It takes everything in me not to hang my head in defeat. And maybe I do, just a little.

Her next words are soft as she steps closer to me. "I've always had a hard time knowing if my relationships are real. If it was the draw of money that made them stick around. And, while that's how it started with us, I thought you and I were more than that. I thought you were the real deal."

I clear my throat. "Emmy, I want to be the real deal for you. I fought like hell not to fall for you, but damn, I couldn't fight it." My arms hang to my side, check still in hand. I lazily lift the check to her and tell her, "I can't accept this money, because I would never expect any kind of money from the woman I've been falling for."

Her breath hitches.

"I want to be real with you, Emmy, for as long as you will have me."

I scan her face, her features, looking for any kind of tell that she wants to be mine. Where I just saw hopefulness moments ago, her eyes are now filled with skepticism.

"That money also bought your secrecy about the Skee-Ball machine. Are you going to spill the beans on that?"

I want to smile and laugh and pull her into my arms, but I hold back. I pull my fingers across my lips, the universal sign of zipping my lips. "Never."

"I might be semi-estranged from my parents, but there will be times that I can't get out of going to King family functions. Those events will be filled with rich and pretentious people. Will you be able to handle that?"

"As long as I've got you by my side, I can handle anything." I'm smiling now and I can tell she's fighting back her own.

"And what if there comes a time that I need you to wear some god-awful sweater vest or *Doctor Who*-esque suit? Will you wear them?" She's clearly fighting back her grin now.

"I'll die before I ever wear a sweater vest."

She hmphs.

"But I can tell you that nothing else matters, because I love you."

She twists her lips then finally says, "Well, lucky you, because I love you, too."

We both stand there for a moment, stupid-ass grins on both our faces. Then I reach out, grab her arms, and haul her in to me.

Our noses nearly touching, I look down into her eyes. "I'm sorry I was a jackass. I can't promise I won't have my moments, but I'll do everything in my power to try to keep you happy, Emmy."

"You don't have to keep me happy. I'll be happy as long as I'm with you," she whispers.

My eyes close briefly at the sound of her hushed words.

"Are you going to kiss me?" I can hear the mirth in her voice.

I smile as I give her what she wants, because making Emmy King happy is my top priority for as long as she will have me.

EPILOGUE

$\mathcal{E}$mmy

FOUR MONTHS LATER ...

"OH, YEAH. GET IN THERE."

I can't help but giggle at Jake.

"Nooo ... it went in the wrong hole." He covers his face with his hand.

"I told you I have the magic touch. These balls are putty in my hands." It's the truth.

"Hmm, yes, you do, baby," he says and nuzzles my neck.

"Ugh, you two are gross. If we couldn't see you playing Skee-Ball right now, we'd be begging you to get a room." Bex sounds disgusted, but when I peek over my shoulder at her, she's smiling. She's perched on the couch next to Kevin.

I snag up the first faux-wooden ball from the machine. And hip-check Jake out of my way.

"We'd be more than happy to get a room." Jake laughs next to me.

"Sure, but in some other apartment. As in not here, in this one." Becca turns up her nose.

"Oh hush, Bex, we're quiet and you know it." I turn to look at her again and she scrunches up her nose.

Jake looks smug and Kevin chuckles, but his focus remains on the halftime report on the television.

Kevin and Jake have taken to coming over to watch sporting events with us. Mostly because our television is bigger, we always have food, and it's easier for Jake to swing by when he's on call or just off work.

Kevin is fun, and he gets along with Bex well enough. I thought briefly that the two of them might hit it off a little too much, but Becca doesn't date younger men. Plus, she has been dating a guy much older than her for the past couple of months. I've not met him yet, which doesn't bother me, but I'm not sure this relationship is going to last a lot longer. She's whip-smart and loves her bartending gig. Marshal has money, and from what she's told me, doesn't love that she tends bar.

Things between Jake and me have been amazing over the past few months. He still works a lot, but on nights when he's on call, he stays over. As long as he has the office-issued cell phone on him, it's not a problem. I also stay at his place occasionally, but it's not Jake's favorite place to be, so we don't go there a lot. Mostly, it's a money pit. He's always having to put his own money into fixing up his unit because his landlord is shitty about doing it himself. I know Jake is itching to get a house. He told me the night we became a real couple that that was the reason he wanted the money. Not that I really had the money then, or now, but I feel bad he ended up not taking the check I gave him. But his pride is important, it wouldn't have made him happy if he had cashed it.

If Jake's happy, I'm happy.

Just as I finish up my turn, there's a knock at the door. Becca announces she will get it and I briefly wonder if this is the moment we will finally meet stuffy Marshal.

It's not though, because I hear a familiar voice. My brother walks down the short hall behind Becca. A surprise visit from Levi; it doesn't happen very often.

"Hey, big brother. What are you doing here?" I walk over and give him a hug. Since the night he came over to tell me he broke off his engagement, I've made it a point to hug him more. It's not something we would normally do but it turns out that we need each other a little more than we thought.

"I was in the building." He drops the words casually and leans past me to shake Jake's hand. Things with Jake and Levi were rocky at first. Jake didn't like the way Levi talked to me the night of the engagement party and he didn't like the way Levi gave him such a hard time about not knowing me, back when we were still a fake couple. Levi didn't love that Jake couldn't handle my upbringing at first. But after a few dinners, they seem to have worked things through.

"Hey, Levi." Jake drops his hand. "I don't think you've met my brother, Kevin." He jerks his head toward the couch.

Kevin stands and shakes his hand and they exchange pleasantries.

"You a Bears fan?" Kevin asks Levi.

"I am but I missed the first half. How are they doing?" They chat about the game for a few minutes. I don't miss the look Levi gives Becca when she slides past him and sits down on the couch next to Kevin. She doesn't sit close, but there are a few other places to sit.

Interesting.

"Levi, so what were you doing in the building?" To my knowledge, he doesn't know anyone else who lives here.

"Ah, yes. Well, I wanted you and Becca here to be the first to say hello to your new neighbor." He performs a little bow.

"What?" He has a great little place a few blocks from here, so I wonder why the move. He'd only lived there for about six months. I peek over at Bex and notice that she's eyeing him with curiosity.

"Yeah, you know my place over on Lexington? Well that was actually mine and Darcy's. I was living there, but it was in both our names. She decided last month that she wanted it. Since I called off the wedding, I decided just to give it to her. Finding a new place and moving was easier than having to deal with her."

"Didn't she also go on the honeymoon?" This comes from Bex. Like me, she never liked Darcy, so she was thrilled when I told her Levi wasn't marrying her. Now that I think about it, maybe it wasn't because she didn't like Darcy.

"Yup." Levi walks over to the couch and sits down next to her. He takes up way too much room when he stretches out and makes himself comfortable.

"So, you're moving into the building?" I try to get him back on track.

"Yeah, right across the hall. I was looking for a two-bedroom and that unit has been vacant for a while. So, Mr. Eastman cut me a deal."

"A deal?" Becca looks at him in disbelief.

"Yeah, it's move-in ready. And he paid half of my down payment."

Kevin whistles and Jake mutters something under his breath.

"So, you bought it?" Becca crosses her arms.

"I sure did. I'm moving in this week." He smiles cockily at her, then looks at me, "Looks like you'll be seeing more of me."

I smile. I love my big brother, and I couldn't think of a better neighbor.

"Well, that's great news, Levi."

With that, we all enjoy a few more beers, chips and salsa, and then watch our team kick butt.

Later, after the game ends, Levi and Kevin leave and Becca heads out for drinks with Marshal. I sit on the couch with my legs draped over Jake's legs, watching a Netflix documentary. Jake looks over at me and I catch his eye and smile back at him.

"I wanted to ask you something." He looks a little nervous.

"What's that?"

"Well, you know I've been looking at houses on Staten Island for several months now, right?"

"Yeah, did you find something?" I hope he did. I don't love that he will be farther away, but it would make him so happy to have his own place. He's looked at a couple of houses, but none of them have "spoken" to him. Plus, he doesn't have the down payment quite yet.

"I didn't but I'm finding that a house on the island isn't what I want anymore."

I arch an eyebrow. "Oh, really?"

"Yeah, I was thinking that it was time to find somewhere else, maybe closer to 425 Madison as well as the Envirogal office."

It takes a moment for me to register what he's saying. I cock my head. "Jake …"

"I was hoping we could find a place together. I know it's entirely too soon to ask you to marry me, but we could at least start thinking about moving in together and maybe see what that looks like." He looks so hopeful.

"Are you for real?"

"I am."

A smile slowly spreads across my face and his follows suit.

"I'd love to move in with you." Happiness bursts through my chest as I tell him he had nothing to worry about.

"Really?" He seems to be just as happy as I feel right now. He leans toward me like he isn't sure he's hearing me correctly.

"Really, really." And I launch myself into his arms. I kiss him and giggle when he finds my ticklish spot.

I lean back from him and tell him, "I'll move in with you, as long as I can bring the Skee-Ball machine."

He laughs deep from his belly, leans in, and kisses my nose.

"Whatever you want, Emmy. Whatever you want."

Thank you for reading BOYFRIEND MAINTENANCE! I hope you enjoyed Emmy and Jake's story. Please consider taking a moment to leave a brief review on Amazon (even one sentence counts!). Reviews are the kind of love that keeps us indie authors alive. Many thanks!

If you loved BOYFRIEND MAINTENANCE, you'll love the rest of the books in the 425 MADISON SERIES. Continue reading for a glimpse of Jameson and Olivia's story, plus details on the other books in the series.

WHAT ABOUT THAT GRILLED CHEESE?

Emmy's Grilled Cheese

What you need:

- 2 slices of thick-cut bread (Emmy likes country white or sourdough)
- Butter
- American cheese from the deli (Emmy always adds a second kind of cheese)
- A flat skillet (a regular skillet works too)
- Spatula

Directions

1. Preheat skillet on medium

2. Butter BOTH sides of each piece of bread.
(Jake is dumb and doesn't like the outside of his bread buttered. He's clearly wrong. Always butter the outside, if you don't, you might as well just use a damn toaster.)

3. Place one or two slices of each type of cheese on the bread to make a sandwich.

4. Let the sandwich grill on medium heat for about 5 minutes before flipping and grilling the other side for about 3 minutes.

5. The grilled cheese is done when you've achieved your desired toastiness. (Emmy likes a nice even grill and isn't a fan of burnt bread. But Jake is still learning and only burns the bread fifty percent of the time now.)

6. Remove from skill and let sit for 2-4 minutes before cutting.
(It's hard, I know, but it's worth it. Jake never waits and hot cheese oozes out the sides and he burns his mouth and fingers. Every flipping time.)

A note on cheese:

It's best to use a cheese that melts well.
(To name a few: American - from the deli, cheddar, jack, mozzarella, and provolone)

When you use two cheeses, they should complement each other.
Here are some suggested cheese combos:

- American and cheddar (Emmy's favorite)
- American and pepper jack (Jake's favorite, though he likes it extra spicy, so try habanero pepper jack)
- cheddar and pepper jack
- American and mozzarella

If you make Emmy's Grilled Cheese at home, please share it on Instagram.

Tag me @Author_LaurenHelms and use the tags #EmmysGrilledCheese & #MaintenanceManFakeBoyfriend

LOVE UNDER CONSTRUCTION - BOOK #6

Love Under Construction, an enemies to lovers romance (book #6) by Aubree
Valentine, releases on 5/16/19.

Jameson
She hates me.
I can't say I blame her, in fact, I thought it was best this way.
That was until I realized just how much I really cared for her.
Now all I want to do is protect her.
It wasn't supposed to be this way.

Olivia
I hate him.
He's always been a thorn in my side.
When my life is flipped upside down, and I'm fighting to stay above water,
things between us shift, and I begin to question everything I thought I knew
about the boy next door.
It wasn't supposed to be this way. I never should have kissed him. It was only a
matter of time.

After all, 425 Madison is the perfect place to fall in love!

Each story is completely standalone, but you'll want to read them all. Trust me.

Don't miss updates about *Boyfriend Maintenance*. Visit www. 425madisonseries.com for all the details.

THE 425 MADISON SERIES

Welcome to 425 Madison Ave, the perfect place to fall in love! Nine delicious romances set in fast-paced & sexy NYC just waiting for you to read.

For more information, visit the series website:
www.425madisonseries.com

Must Love Coffee by Leigh Lennon
Book #1
A Second Chance Romance
Release: 1/31/19

Let Me Love You by MK Moore
Book #2
A Best Friend's Sibling Romance
Release: 2/21/19

Just Swipe Right by Allie York
Book #3
A Love Triangle Romance

Release: 3/14/19

Two for Holding by Kay Gordon
Book #4
A Sports Romance
Release: 4/4/19

Boyfriend Maintenance by Lauren Helms
Book #5
A Fake Relationship Romance
Release: 4/25/19

Love Under Construction by Aubree Valentine
Book #6
A Enemies to Lovers Romance
Release: 5/16/19

Back For More by Sylvia Kane
Book #7
A Brother's Best Friend Romance
Release: 6/6/19

Accidentally in Love by Katy Ames
Book #8
An Ugly Duckling Romance
Release: 6/27/19

Sightseeing in Manhattan by C. Lesbirel
Book #9
A Soul Mate Romance
Release: 7/18/19

ALSO BY LAUREN HELMS

Gamer Boy Series

Level Me Up (Morgan & Dex) - Gamer Boy #1

One More Round (Gia & Simon) - Gamer Boy #2

Game All Night (Ruby & Link) - Gamer Boy #3

Gamer Boy #4 (Bernie & Wade) - coming 2019

STAY CONNECTED

Come join my reader group, Lauren's Romance Game Changers over on Face-book! - https://www.facebook.com/groups/LsRomGameChangers/

Stay up-to-date on new release information, exclusive content, and more! Sign up for my newsletter today: http://bit.ly/newsletter_LH

I'm always looking for awesome readers to join my review team. Interested? Sign up here: https://goo.gl/forms/tVkydhJgjh8gDcSn2

- Facebook - http://bit.ly/Facebook_LH
- Twitter - http://bit.ly/Twitter_LH
- Instagram - http://bit.ly/Insta_LH
- Amazon - https://amzn.to/2IqJ68N
- BookBub - http://bit.ly/BookBub_LH
- Goodreads - http://bit.ly/GoodR_LH
- Books + Main - http://bit.ly/BooksMain_LH
- Pinterest - http://bit.ly/Pinterest_LH

ACKNOWLEDGMENTS

As always, I couldn't have made Boyfriend Maintenance what it is without my team of VIPs. There's a group of people that I have come to rely on every time I write and publish a book. I'll keep this super short, because honestly, once you write one of these acknowledgment sections, it's hard to come up with new material.

Robert, I love you.

To my little monster's, thank you for making sure I'm always on the brink of insanity.

Cassie Graham, thank you for all your help when it came to plotting this bad boy. We have some mad plotting skills when we work together. I look forward to writing our book someday, which is hopefully sooner rather than later. I also want to mention that you are now obligated to alpha/beta read every book I write from this point on. #SorryNotSorry.

Aubree Valentine and Allie York, both of you helped me develop Jake and Emmy's story when I was stuck. You both mean the world to me.

Leigh, M.K., Allie, Kay, Aubree, Sylvia, Katy, and Claire: you all took a chance with me and this journey of ours. Thank you for making it amazing.

Laura, Joy, Debbie, and Kristina: thank you for all the invaluable feedback on my story. Your support and excitement gives me the confidence I need to send this book baby of mine out into the world.

Lastly, to all you amazing bloggers and readers: without you, all my words would go unread. Thank you for all your support of my books as well as the whole 425 Madison series.

ABOUT THE AUTHOR

Lauren Helms has forever been an avid reader from the beginning. After starting a book review website that catapulted her fully into the book world, she knew that something was missing. Lauren decided to take the plunge and write her first novel. While working for a video game strategy guide publisher, she decided to mix what she knew best--video games and romance. She decided to take the plunge and joined NaNoWriMo and a month later, she had her first draft.

Join my Facebook group!
Lauren's Romance Game Changers
www.authorlaurenhelms.com